15/9/25

LONGSHOT

LONGSHOT

LONGSHOT

AVERY BLAKE
JOHNNY B. TRUANT

STERLING & STONE

To YOU, the reader.

Thank you for taking a chance on us.

Thank you for your support.

Thank you for the emails.

Thank you for the reviews.

Thank you for reading and joining us on this road.

ONE

The Gambler

ON THE DAY Las Vegas burned, John Abbott, the Gambler, decided to let it ride.

He had a gun in his room's safe, which he'd brought for the higher-drama way this could end. That plan took a back seat when, after four days at the Lucky's blackjack tables, John finally won enough that they gave him a nicer suite, one with windows from which he could almost — but not really — see the Strip.

He was also given a key — not a keycard, as Lucky's was a brass and tumblers sort of place — that opened what the front desk referred to as "the High Rollers' Spa." But Maria, the maid he met before she jumped off the roof, said the housekeeping staff just called that one "the pool without shit in it."

John had his doubts about this claim. Even if there wasn't literal feces in the High Rollers' pool, there was some crap for sure. He'd peeked into the dingy room and considered the hot tub. Once. But if there were still places where you could get a Legionnaires' Disease contact buzz, D-list casinos like Lucky's were it. Even the high falutin' spa looked like soup in the making.

Shortly before Maria became a stain on the concrete deck, before the rioting started and that gang of improbable Road Warrior types came through in Big Daddy Roth hotrods, John changed his mind about the gun. He found a street dealer to buy an overdose of pills from instead. The gun, by then, was clearly disrespectful. He'd hold onto it just in case, but it was a dick move so far as suicides went.

John hadn't thought the gun method through. He'd bought hollow-points from a friend he was ashamed to know because he wanted to be sure. But, after meeting Maria, he realized how inconsiderate that was. *Hollow points? Really?* He'd paint half the room in blood and brain.

Once, in college, his buddy Searle propelled an

orange into the communal bathroom using a home-made canon. Dorm housekeeping had found pulp in unusual places for the rest of the year. Even if they could get all the gray matter out of the air holes in the TV and track down the aerosolized blood that was bound to waft into the vents, who's to say a guest six months from now might not go for the Gideon Bible and find parts of his tongue in the drawer?

Everyone forgot about the tongue, but John was willing to bet it'd go, too. Legend said a hollow round at point-blank range made a hole large enough to reach through and shake hands. There was bound to be some inconvenience for the maids, and really, they were just hardworking folks trying to make ends meet.

The issue was growing increasingly moot. The end of the world was really ruining things. On the first day, John lost as usual. It was only on his second afternoon at Lucky's — after the big announcement came from the sky, and everyone started to claw out their eyes and scream and cry and embark on desperate, traffic-choked missions to find family members who might already be dead — that John started winning.

Another tease from the universe. Big John

Abbott finally winning for five seconds before death beams consumed the planet. He'd played on anyway, waiting for the casino staff to shut things down. Fortunately or unfortunately, the CEO was dragged into the street, throat-slit, and robbed. After that, nobody really knew what to do.

The entertainment VP seemed to decide that there were still people in the hotel, so the showgirls might as well perform. Some of the dancers fled, but more than half stayed. John cynically imagined rifts between fathers and daughters that caused so many to stick around in the city of sin instead of seeking family. Gaming heads, without upper management, weren't sure enough that the bosses were really gone to kill the casino floor, so they kept right on playing. The pit bosses followed whatever the gaming heads said to do, and the dealers followed the pit bosses' orders.

The burning cleared out a lot more folks. Interestingly, their departures only hardened the resolve of those who remained. The more people ran off in terror, the more those who'd stayed behind were determined to stick their fingers in their ears and close their eyes, playing Vivaldi on the deck while the Titanic came closer and closer to kissing the sweet ocean floor.

He suspected it boiled down to denial. But after the Strip burned and John suddenly *was* able to see it from his window, he started to think cognitive dissonance might explain things better. If you learned that alien ships were on their way and *still* kept gambling, you couldn't really change your mind a day later. If you did that, you'd have to admit you were being irrational when you stayed the first day. Nobody wanted to publicly bet against their own consistency.

So the casino stayed open, and some of the people stayed along with some of the staff. By the time the Strip was ashes, and the gangs were still avoiding Lucky's ramshackle part of town, it felt almost like providence. Where else was there to go for the already-desperate? Guests at Lucky's had a system. They couldn't beat the Bellagio or the MGM Grand, but gambler's logic said Lucky's odds were looser. If you believed that, you tended to believe the world-ending might not be your problem. *Everyone* was lucky at Lucky's, after all.

John, on the other hand, wasn't so deluded. He didn't have a gambling problem, at least not beyond the hundreds of thousands of dollars — plus one wife and two kids — he'd lost. Nor did he have any other psychological issues to deal with. He really only had that history with his absentee mother. And all the anger at his deadbeat father. Also, deep insecurity, depression, insomnia, intense self-loathing, and suicidal ideation.

Other than that, John was tip-top, damage-free. He wasn't staying because he was pretending all was well in the world. Nope — he stayed because he was on one hell of a roll. He won, and won, and won, and won … and when Day Six came, and the ships started landing, and gaming finally shut down for lack of staff and common sense, John started asking single men at the deserted bar if they'd like to play any game where money was exchanged, shoving aside any notions that money might no longer mean anything and that the best winning streak of his life was for naught. It was depressing.

Suicide no longer felt so important, though. He worried at night because the alternative was fretting about the mothership they'd seen heading west, and the smaller burnished-metal spheres the news called "shuttles" plaguing the Vegas airspace like locusts.

John worried not that he'd considered killing himself — that was logical, as his death made more sense than his life ever had — but that he'd stopped considering it. Or *postponed* it.

That should feel like an improvement, but John

suspected it was the opposite. Family hadn't given him the will to live. Work hadn't given him the will to live. Ambition or grand thoughts of "dinging the universe," if he'd ever had any, wouldn't have given him the will to live. But *gambling?* Boy howdy.

The coming apocalypse had just ended the best streak of his life. If he'd been able to keep it up, he could've won back everything he'd ever lost. His attitude of "Fuck it, bet everything, I'm offing myself soon anyway," had made him fearless at the tables. He'd wager it all on the dumbest long-shots.

But those long-shots kept paying off, and every time they did, John would find a new lousy bet and let it ride. Kenny Rogers said you shouldn't count your money when sitting at the table. John was superstitious enough of a gambler to be wary of counting it at all, ever.

Still, he might be up thirty grand or more. Ten-to-one that and he'd be at 300K. Ten-to-one *that* and he'd be at three million.

With three million dollars and all his problems solved, Linda would take him back.

He'd be able to buy new everything for the kids to make up for everything he pawned. He wouldn't need his job back. He'd be able to start one of the many companies he always planned.

And if it was a risk? Who cared! With that three million bucks practically in his pockets already, he'd have plenty to spare.

Then it could end.

Things would finally be better.

There'd be no reason to kill himself. This hot streak, if John could just find a way to keep it going, would turn everything around.

A slim, attractive woman, with hard brown eyes that lent a look of loathing to her face, sat beside him at the empty hotel bar.

"I got a new one. You wanna hear it?"

John looked over. Of course, he was attracted to the woman, but doing anything about it would be like putting on red boxers, getting into the ring with a bull, then bending over.

"No," he said.

"Man walks into a casino. He meets a pretty dancer with big tits and says, 'Can I buy you a drink?' She counts his chips and says, 'I like you for your personality.'"

John waited for more. Then he said, "That's not a joke."

Kristina reached over the bar, grabbed a glass and a bottle, then poured herself a finger of Scotch before giving him a once-over. "Yes, it is."

John considered getting up and leaving, but she'd just follow him.

"I didn't ask to buy her a drink," John said without looking over.

"Where *is* Rainbow Brite, anyway?" she asked.

"How should I know?"

"I assumed she was under the bar, looking for money behind your zipper." Kristina made a show of looking down. "Nope. Maybe she's upstairs in your bed, rolling around in your solid life prospects."

"I was just being friendly."

"Uh-huh. Speaking of being friendly with everyone, even if they don't have blowjob lips, how are things with Cruella?"

"Do you mean Margaret?"

Kristina sipped her scotch beside him.

He chanced a look. She was maybe five-three and stunning when the effort was there, though it did seem hard to come by. Like with insects, sometimes the pretty little ones were deadliest.

"Whatever. You just know she's got a Dalmatian coat in her room."

His best option right now was keeping his mouth shut. You didn't verbally spar with Kristina Fine. He'd seen a few of her videos on YouTube.

She didn't cut hecklers from her routines. She cut routines and kept only the hecklers. Her *Best Of Dickholes* had been fifteen of his favorite minutes before meeting her, but now he was one of the dick-holes, and that made their encounter equal parts awkward and uncomfortable.

She was fast on her feet and a little too fluid with the spoken word to be tested. Trying to win a conversational point against her was like playing Pat-a-Cake with a ninja.

"She just seemed a little down," John said, though Kristina had already moved on, and now he was just squirting fuel on her flame.

"Cruella? I think that's just how her face is."

"Lisa."

"Probably sad because she lost her picture books. And before she found out what the Hungry Hungry Caterpillar was going to eat next!"

"She's twenty-three."

"Ah. You've foiled me. Of course, you'd know. What's her star sign?"

"Why are you such an asshole?" he asked.

Kristina shrugged, unperturbed. "I don't know. It works for me."

She shifted on her stool, body toward him. Her posture changed, becoming softer. In something closer to a whisper, she said, "Listen. They can't possibly let us live much longer, right? They'll *Independence Day* this shit any moment now. Truth is, maybe I'm a little jealous of Lisa. She was probably a cheerleader while I was being kicked around with the goths kids. If the world's going to end …" Long pause. Knowing eyes, lined with dark shadow. "Wanna go out with a bang?"

She was smiling. He hadn't seen that before. "Seriously?"

She bit her lip.

"Okay," he said.

Her coy act snapped like a twig. She turned front again, sipped her Scotch, and said, "Knew it. Pervert."

John walked away.

He'd paced the casino a thousand times by now, and in truth, there just weren't many places to go. That made this pointless for him and delightful for his pursuer. The floors above One were nothing but rooms, and an improvised explosive two days earlier had shaken the entire building, dropping every key from a pegboard in the office onto the floor.

They weren't labeled. What kind of a system was that? It meant every room other than those they already had keys to were effectively closed forever, making for some extremely boring exploration.

"I guess I don't blame you," Kristina said from his five o'clock position. He couldn't entirely see her. It was as if his self-doubt had taken physical form, linked arms with the devil on his shoulder, and decided to trail him for sport. "She's pretty."

"All I did was say hello."

"And hey, you're not bad looking yourself."

It sounded almost sincere. John didn't reply.

"You'd make a cute couple. Like my cousin and his blow-up doll."

John kept walking.

"Hey," Kristina said, undaunted. "You wanna hear something interesting?"

"No."

"Really. I'm serious."

"What?"

"You know Dennis?"

"Yeah. He and me are lifetime friends."

"*He and me,*" she repeated. "You must have killed it on the SAT."

John entered the dim section of the casino, where all the slots were dark. Nobody he interacted with knew why the power was still on, even halfway. Lucky's had been at partial capacity when the

Astral announcement came, then emptied to maybe ten percent after six days passed, and the alien ships were soaring over Vegas.

That culling process had left only the hardened among them — those who'd decided to stay simply because they had nowhere better to go. A few days of alien occupation — plus roving gangs, which they'd had a lot of since the burning — had thinned their number even further, scaring off all but the truly lost, suicidal, deluded, or nihilistic. Well, except for John. He stayed because Lucky's construction was ancient and nearly bombproof, and also he had money to win and a gun to stick in his mouth the second things turned south.

John guessed there were maybe fifty people within the walls, but the casino had been built in wings, and already there was inter-wing tension. People couldn't stop forming tribes, and tribes couldn't stop suspecting and warring with each other. If he went to the convention center tribe or the baccarat/sports betting tribe to ask about the power, he might end up with his head on a pike.

"Anyway," Kristina continued from his heels, "he and me had a talk. Do you know what he did before he was a pit boss?"

John entered the men's restroom.

Kristina followed, of course. "You thought Lisa was going to be in here, didn't you?"

"This is the men's room," John said.

She pointed. "Try the stalls. She might have her feet up."

John walked back out without peeing. He didn't actually have to go. He was just looking for a way to lose his tail, but the only way to ditch anyone here was to go to the one place nobody wanted to go. *Outside*.

So far, they'd been as lucky as John's lucky streak. Those raiding and destroying Vegas seemed to have decided Lucky's was too sad to have anything worth looting. It wasn't a perception he wanted to spoil.

As he left, Kristina made a disappointed noise about peeking at his johnson.

They emerged then continued a clockwise loop. There was another way, past all the ten-dollar slots, but that led to the convention center. As unstable as John's accidental group was, supposedly, the convention center creeps were much worse. They'd come for business, and it took a certain kind of businessperson to book their conference at Lucky's. They probably ate their dead, just because it was easier.

After a moment, they stepped from the dim section and back into the light.

"Hey, wait up," Kristina said.

John walked faster.

She started to jog. "You know, I'm going to give up on you eventually."

"Good."

"I'll bet you've never had angry sex. I'll bet you've never once done some good ol' fashioned fucking and punching."

John didn't bite. Most of the group was ahead in its default spot — a cluster of ordinary tables in the most brightly lit area. If you focused on other people inside that little bubble, it was almost possible to forget that half the world was running from A to B while the other half raced from B to A. The area was far enough from the windows that they could all pretend they were on a little casino vacay together. Convincing enough that whenever she sat down here, Kristina kept asking Lisa the Showgirl to get them drinks.

"I didn't tell you about Dennis," she said.

John walked faster, but now they must look comical. He finally slowed. She seemed to take it as a victory.

"Before he was a Pit Boss, he was a doctor."

"And?"

"But don't you see? Maybe he could remove the stick from Todd's ass!"

John spun around, confronting her. "Okay. For real. You need to stop making fun of Todd."

"For real?" she mocked.

"Do you know why he drives an armored car?"

"Hold on. I can think of a funny answer to that."

"Because he used to be a cop." John considered going on with his guessing game, asking Kristina why the man was no longer a cop, but the question would be a mistake and cost him his temporary control over the conversation. "He was called to a bank robbery, but when they showed up, the robber guys panicked and began shooting. They killed his partner and ran. Cops outside got in cars to chase the shooter, but Todd sort of snapped, broke procedure and went after him. Got himself shot, and he nearly died. I think most of the time, the guy wishes he had. He's got PTSD so bad, he can't even sleep."

Kristina nodded. "So maybe I don't ask him to play Tag."

"Really? No compassion at all?"

"*Compassion?*" Her sarcastic echo was replaced

by something more biting. "You didn't just tell me that so we could all give him group hugs. You're worried he'll snap."

Sort of. John had spied Todd cutting lines of wallpaper into long strips using a Rambo-length knife. He might have already snapped.

"Don't lecture me." Her tone said he'd pushed too far, and she wasn't playing anymore. "Just because everyone looks to you like some kind of leader doesn't mean we all want one."

"You could leave," he said.

"*You* could leave."

They were staring each other down when Joanna, the Bride, started to scream.

TWO

The Groom

SHE REALLY IS WONDERFUL, Lawrence thought as he considered Joanna standing over by the roulette table. It was too bad her biggest goal, in the wake of the alien invasion, was to not die while still married to him. That hurt a lot, but Lawrence wasn't prepared to hold it against her. She was too wonderful for that.

Joanna, in Lawrence's opinion, was "wonderful" in a holistic way — or really in a way that transcended merely *holistic*, since *holistic* just meant "as a whole," and as such could apply to everything from holistic health to the entirety of a car's operation rather than only a single one of its systems.

Joanna's wonderfulness was all-encompassing. It was a law, like the law of gravity, the cosine law he'd learned in high school trigonometry. He would never have said she was a goddess — that was too creepy — but he wouldn't have denied it, either.

He'd written poems about her. Long, embarrassing stanzas full of predictable rhymes that Lawrence suspected were more pretentious than good — but that didn't matter because he'd never share them anyway. He'd had fantasies since they were fourteen and both lived on Sycamore Street, that one day he'd win her heart from whichever beau she had at the time by reading her his poems.

They were cheesy, sure. But you could say that about every outspoken declaration of love these days. She'd see the sincerity of his words despite all that, and the adoration Joanna felt for him would overwhelm any perception of cheesiness, and afterward, the two of them would embark upon an age-old romance of the sort that Shakespeare would have been proud to write about.

Young Lawrence could see himself at the window, upwardly professing his love. He imagined years of courtship in which he'd never fail to bring her flowers, or send cards, or write letters, or all the other ridiculous things people in movies did when enamored. Theirs could be a love for the ages, as far as Lawrence was concerned.

Except that it hadn't even lasted a day. Scientists had announced those giant spheres headed Earth's way just after Joanna had, yet again, thrown Lawrence into the Friend-Zone while begging for his support after her latest breakup. Her problem was that she kept dating men who weren't Lawrence, and *his* problem was that Joanna had no idea how he felt despite all that shoulder-crying.

The Astral announcement had opened her eyes to new possibilities for the first time ever … what with death around the corner and all. When Lawrence suggested they head to Vegas and party until the end of the world to forget her troubles along with all the sudden interplanetary ails, she'd agreed with enthusiasm that felt like more than friendship.

It had been a week since then — a horrific terror-filled week that brought them closer together right up through the aliens' arrival.

Over that past week, things had changed for the better. They'd sat too close and brushed hands too often, and just last night, he'd finally stolen a kiss. She was drunk, and he was drunk, so there was no reason not to come clean about his affections.

They were two of fewer than a dozen people holed up together, waiting for the inevitable. To

Lawrence, that meant all bets were off. He'd told her the truth, and she'd blushed, flattered and pleased. She'd touched his arm, said he was so very, very sweet.

And it turned out that Dennis, the Pit Boss, was ordained because he sometimes filled in for Elvis at the casino chapel, so on impulse, they'd decided to get married.

Lawrence figured it was the dawn after a cold, dark night — that his pining was finally over. Joanna, however, felt differently by the sober dawn. She said he'd read the signs wrong. She hadn't *given* any, in fact. Instead, he'd invented a fantasy and forced them both into believing it.

She'd been too drunk to know what she was doing and was furious that he'd pushed them into marriage anyway. He'd hoodwinked her. Taken advantage. Manipulated her while she was feeling low. Caught her on the rebound like she always knew he'd planned to. Oh, yes, she *knew*.

They'd been married for less than twenty-four hours now, and the cynics were apparently right — marriage really did change everything. Now they weren't even talking. She hated him. And still, he couldn't stop watching her by the roulette table, casually spinning the big wheel like she could never do in an operational casino. Try that without an alien invasion, and security came to break a leg.

Joanna was the perfect woman, despite it all. Despite the fact that she treated their drunken marriage like a growth she'd only now noticed and would have to wait in disgust before it could be effectively removed. She'd been a friend for most of his life. She'd seen through his obesity and been a rock through his weight loss. She was, as far as Lawrence was concerned, the kindest, sweetest, and most interesting woman in the world despite this new hatred for him. Never mind that she was beautiful. Joanna was worth more than her beauty.

He'd thought there was nothing worse than treading water, with her ignorant of the torch he had never stopped carrying. But Lawrence was wrong — this was a thousand times worse. At least there'd been hope in the pining days. Now, he had nothing.

"You're better off," said a voice.

Lawrence looked over and saw Todd.

"I told you yesterday, man. Girls like that, they put you in a box. I told you she was drunk. I told you she wasn't really into you."

That was ridiculous. Joanna had always been "into" Lawrence. She just hadn't realized it.

"I have to tell you something as a friend," Todd said, moving closer.

Was Todd a friend? They'd known each other six days and were nothing alike. Todd had a square jaw, a shaved head, and eyes that even Lawrence, who'd never had gay leanings, found dead sexy.

Lawrence, on the other hand, was an ex-programmer who'd been laid off first because he was the most expendable. He'd turned out all right. People said he was handsome now and had been so even when he'd been fat, but not in the smoldering way men like Todd were. Or, for that matter, know-it-all John Abbott.

Lawrence had deeper virtues. He was kind, intelligent, well-read, and stable despite the layoff because he'd spent prudently and never stopped saving. Todd had been a cop and still carried a firearm, whereas Lawrence had pulled the trigger just once before complaining about soreness from the rifle's kick for days.

They didn't really have the common ground to be friends ... but alien invasions made strange bedfellows.

"What?" Lawrence asked.

"She's into Abbott."

Lawrence knew that. She hadn't thought to

remove the gumball-budget ring he'd smashed-and-grabbed from the gift shop — the band read, *I got lucky at Lucky's* — so there she was brushing strands of beautiful hair from her face while gazing at the Gambler's approach.

Lawrence supposed he liked the guy, though he didn't want to. Not when he kept making Joanna's expression all dewy.

"Why would you say that?" Lawrence asked.

"Because it's true," Todd answered.

"I know it's true. Come on, man. Have a heart."

"I don't want to see you making a fool of yourself. I've had plenty of friends who were made fools by girls."

"We probably only have a few hours left to live, anyway."

Todd leaned back and looked left. There were windows that way, and Todd seemed to be checking them. "No new fires on the Strip for forty-eight hours. And I've not heard any muscle cars in at least that long. Everyone acts like they're here to kill us, but man, think about it. Why? Why would you do that?"

Lawrence was just going with majority opinion. It's not like he was responsible for thinking up this sequence of events. Besides, it seemed wise to go with the worst-case scenario. That way, being wrong might still lead to a pleasant surprise.

In about half of the alien movies Lawrence had seen, the aliens came to conquer. In the other half, they came to study and maybe make peace. But in the latter films, the extraterrestrials didn't usually abduct people *en masse* like this crew apparently already had, and from what he heard, there were no signs of slowing down.

Even a few famous people had been abducted, according to the online rumor mill, such as it still existed.

Why abduct if they wanted peace?

Although Lawrence had to admit it could go either way. Technically, none of the ships had even landed, and there weren't any aliens on the ground. They didn't know if they were big and black, small and green, or some sort of gooey creature in between.

Todd nudged him. "Look. She's leaving. Maybe she's *not* into Abbott."

As if Lawrence hadn't seen, Todd thrust his chin toward the Gambler, now approaching with that tiny Comedian on his heels. Joanna had seen him and was now heading in the opposite direction.

It could mean what Todd said or nothing.

Maybe it meant Joanna was finding a corner where she could lure Abbott and quietly — or perhaps loudly — flog his bone.

This time, it would be adultery.

"I, uh …" Lawrence liked Todd, but the dude was a bummer. He had a wife and college-age daughter who lived on the Vegas outskirts but had already decided both were dead. He kept pointing out all that could definitely would go wrong. Lawrence was pessimistic enough without him. "I need to ask Jeremy something."

Todd was so unperturbed, he might not have even heard. He'd slipped a knife from his belt and started dragging the blade across his forearm like a cutter without the commitment. "Sure, sure. You do you."

Now that Joanna was gone, Lawrence felt safe approaching the group without fear of being shouted down — or, on one memorable occasion, hours ago, getting accused of rape. Which was unfair, as so far as he could tell, they hadn't consummated their ill-conceived marriage. If Lawrence was going to be falsely accused, shouldn't he at least get to see his new wife naked? Or touch more than a forearm?

Jeremy Barnett was in a big leather armchair, his white hair perfectly combed. Even just sitting and waiting, the man's charisma was brighter than neon. It had to be, Lawrence supposed — all performers of all stripes had to have charisma. Barnett was wearing a dark blue suit with a matching tie in a full Windsor knot over a light blue dress shirt. Lawrence was in his last clean pair of clothes — a loud Hawaiian shirt and shorts that were either too short or too long, he couldn't decide.

To be fair, Jeremy made everyone feel under-dressed. His engagement at Lucky's was months' long, so of course, he could still be a clotheshorse, even during the apocalypse.

"Lawrence! Have a seat," Barnett said, a broad smile on his still-handsome features. Jesus. Even the old men here made Lawrence feel like a troll. But the guy was all right. Barnett, unlike everyone else besides Joanna, didn't call him Larry.

"Why's everyone down here?" Lawrence asked.

"I can't speak for everyone, but power's out in my room. With the sun setting, it's—"

"What time is it?"

"—too dark to see," he finished. Then, taking his time, Barnett rolled one wrist to look at his watch. "It's almost seven."

"And the power's out?"

"Not here, no."

"Well, yeah. I mean—"

"I don't ask questions, Lawrence. I stopped asking questions when I turned seventy. Life is so much easier this way."

Lawrence admired the man's calm. But then again, he had much less time on his clock than the others did. Except for Margaret, of course — Barnett only had three years on her. His calm manner, his attention to wardrobe despite the circumstances … it all projected a false normality that Lawrence was eager to believe.

"So, you're here because the power's out."

"I am, yes."

"Not the others?"

"I can't speak for the others. I do know we had a fly-by today. Maybe that's made them uneasy."

"A fly-by? You mean one those big silver things?"

"Not like the one over Vail or Moab, no. I mean—"

"So, it was one of the smaller ones?"

Barnett waited a blink for Lawrence to finish his interruption, then proceeded without hurry. "I mean one of the smaller ships."

"What did it do?"

"Nothing that I saw, but Mr. Cross says it stopped, hovered, and seemed to look through his window."

"No."

"Yes," said Barnett.

"What does he think it wanted?"

"Try as I might, I cannot be Amerigo Cross. However, I'm sure Mr. Cross himself could answer that question for you."

Lawrence looked. As usual, Cross was alone, standing far away from the others, drawing attention to himself by pretending he couldn't care less. It was a physical form of passive aggression. A way of saying, *Look at me but also stop staring.*

Maybe that was a career hazard. Magicians — especially close-up performers like Cross — could only do their work if they could draw attention to one place while avoiding it elsewhere.

"I—" Lawrence began.

But then Joanna was screaming, from somewhere far beyond the slots.

Lawrence leapt to his feet. He ran, passing even

Dennis and Todd, who were close enough to respond immediately.

I'm the last person Joanna wants right now.

An uninvited thought, devastating and immediate.

Screw that. I'm saving her whether she wants it or not.

The second thought was much better. Joanna was sensible and still his friend, so, of course, she would thank him for it.

He ran into Lisa first. Both women had passed the gaming floor and entered the lit part of the restaurant. He hated the vulnerability cast upon their little group by the restaurant's wide bank of windows. He'd lobbied for boards and nails to cover them if only to hide their presence from the nutballs and looters, irritated because everyone knew casinos weren't even supposed to have any windows. But this place was ancient, a rare survivor from the days when the mob strolled the floor in plain sight.

They'd been fortunate so far, but if Barnett was right and the alien ships were looking through windows, this entire side of the hotel was a giant liability.

But Lawrence saw nothing in the twilight outside.

He knew Joanna was spooked because she allowed him to sidle up between her and Lisa without shouting for him to leave … or at least divorce her, maybe get his head out of his delusional ass.

"Did someone scream?"

Joanna ignored him. "Did you see that?"

Lisa didn't reply.

Lawrence turned his head and saw her nodding. "What did you see?"

Lisa also ignored him. "It was a dog."

"It was too big to be a dog," Joanna replied.

"What was?" Lawrence asked.

"It was a *tiger.*" Strangely, Lisa sounded relieved.

Joanna shook her head. "There's no way it was a tiger."

"It was totally a tiger! From a stage act!"

"What stage act?" Joanna asked.

"I don't know. Siegfried and Roy?"

"Roy's dead. Has been forever."

"He is?" Lisa looked genuinely surprised.

Joanna looked at her, and for the first time, seemed to notice Lawrence between them. "You work here," she told Lisa.

"Not with tigers."

"I don't even think they let people work with tigers anymore. PETA."

"What's this about tigers?" Lawrence asked.

Joanna regarded him with withering hatred, and it occurred to Lawrence that he'd done what he'd come here to do. Just not the way he wanted. Instead of soothing Joanna or solving whatever was wrong, his presence alone had eliminated her fear.

Presto-change-o. Terror becomes loathing.

Amerigo Cross couldn't have done it better.

"We saw something take that maid's body," Lisa said.

"What do you mean, 'something'?" Lawrence was already nervous.

There was a golf ball in his throat and a brick in his gut. That poor maid had never been cleaned up after her swan dive from the roof. Despite the sacrilege of leaving her, heading outside and into the riots felt far too dangerous.

By the time the rampaging slowed, and the fires were finally dying, most of them had forgotten. Lawrence, for one, had been happy to leave her if it kept people from coming over to gaze out the windows — and be seen by God-knew-who. Or what.

"She means *something*, Lawrence," Joanna spat. "And she means *the maid's body*. Get it?"

"She's not out there anymore?" It was hard to see through the glass. The illumination behind the slots versus the growing dark outside had turned it reflective.

"That's part of the whole 'took it' thing." Joanna's manner was so unnecessarily bitchy that Lawrence almost forgot his undying adoration and snapped back.

But Lisa spoke first. "A big black thing just snatched it."

"How could you tell?"

"It ran through the light."

Lawrence looked.

A single deck light was still glowing, curious as the scattered illumination inside. He couldn't see where the maid had been, only what looked like a spotlight on empty concrete. And a pool of blood.

"Maybe it was a dog," said Lawrence.

Joanna replied without looking at him. "Thanks for the mansplanation. We hadn't thought of that."

Lawrence approached the glass, wishing now that he'd taken his time rushing over. He could hear some of the others coming from behind, including the low, let's-keep-it-cool voice of The Gambler. He was caught between two undesirable options — putting his face to the window and maybe finding himself staring at a nightmare or waiting for Abbott to win the applause. Right in front of Joanna.

He chose the first, cupping hands around his eyes to see. He was sure they were wrong. The patio was to the rear and fronted vacant lots. Nobody would come to steal a body when they hadn't come to pilfer anything inside — especially not now that she'd been out there for days in the sun.

Margaret spoke first. She had gravel in her voice from decades of smoking, a sound that in her youth had probably been sexy.

"What happened?"

"Joanna and Lisa saw a dog or something. They say it took the maid's body."

"What body?" asked Amerigo Cross.

"Some maid jumped from the roof." Todd made the sign of the cross, but it seemed almost comedic.

"Her name was Maria," Abbott clarified.

Joanna said, "It wasn't a dog."

Lisa shrugged. "Maybe a big dog."

"Probably a lot of loose dogs." Lawrence forced himself to stay near the glass. He was the center of attention, for now, the hero for once. It was tempting fate, but if he moved away, they'd all look to Abbott again. "People ran out of Vegas before the Strip burned, and I'll bet it's half-empty out there now."

"It wasn't a dog," Joanna repeated.

"Dogs like meat. Flesh is meat." Amerigo spoke as if reading a fortune.

"Like a Doberman." Lisa tried again. "Or a Great Dane."

"You saw how it moved," Joanna told her. "Dogs don't move like that."

"Then what the hell was it?" someone asked. Lawrence didn't know who.

"Come on," said Dennis, the Pit Boss. "Obviously, something was going to take it. It's gross but nothing to freak out about. This is the desert. There are coyotes, wolves."

"Wolves?" Amerigo repeated the word as though it had aroused him.

"Wild dogs, domestic dogs, bobcats …" Dennis started a list.

"Bobcats are small," Todd interjected.

"Chupacabras …" said the Comedian.

"Goddammit, it wasn't anything like that!" Joanna snapped. "It was—"

Four or five people exclaimed at once.

Flashes of fear, there and then gone.

But Joanna and Lisa were primed, so their screams longest and loudest.

Lawrence scrambled back from the window, upending chairs on his way.

He could still see the shape. The glare from the interior lights obscured it as much as the dark outside, but still, every one of them saw something just beyond the apron. About the size of an SUV, pure black and visible only as highlights and negative space.

The thing was just sitting there. As if it'd always been.

At first, Lawrence thought it was entirely still — *so* still, he was starting to believe it might be a trick of the light, turning a fountain statue into something macabre.

But then he saw the way the highlights shifted in regular rhythm, sliding in tiny arcs up and down what must be a polished black surface.

As if the creature was breathing.

"What the hell is *that?*" asked the Pit Boss.

"Jesus Christ," said Kristina, her voice stunned into reluctant sincerity. "That thing looks like the Batmobile."

To Lawrence, it seemed like an enormous insect. A cockroach the size of a car.

The thing opened a vague black hole that was, in better light, probably its mouth. Something fell from the maw then rolled into the light.

The maid's head.

Lisa screamed even louder than the last time. She screamed. And screamed. And screamed.

Eventually, Todd came up from behind to put a hand over her mouth, making the Showgirl's already-big blue eyes look downright protuberant. She struggled, but he hissed for her to settle. They all waited, the entire assembly afraid to move.

"I don't think it heard her," said Barnett.

But he was wrong. When the beast turned to face them, they could see only teeth. Concentric rings inside a cavernous trap. Each miniature blade was clearly visible … not thanks to the porch light above, but due to a deep blue glow that seemed to crackle with a current from somewhere in the creature's throat.

"Quiet," said Abbott, just above a whisper. *"Don't move."*

The mouth roared loud enough to shake the glass and make the ground tremble.

More people screamed, and Lawrence, though he couldn't be sure, thought he was one of them.

They startled and jumped, but before anyone could run, the thing leapt into the shadows.

There was no relief in watching it go.

Only the premonition of fear.

THREE

The Comedian

WHILE ALL THE sad sacks in the lobby bitched and moaned about the … What was the phrase? … the *impossible horrible creature* outside, Kristina decided to take a stroll. But not outside. There was a fine line between sarcastic and suicidal, and Kristina had always walked it like a tightrope. It was the best way to gather new material for her routine, and the only way to avoid taking a stand.

Taking stands was the best way to end up disappointed. It was better to avoid (amateur) or mock (pro) the things that mattered than to pursue them, because that way you could watch and see what happened while staying safe. It was a bit like sniping from a pillbox — you could get them, but they couldn't get you.

She walked through the east corridor and all its darkness, up a level, through the second floor, then toward a distant stairwell where she could cut back down again.

Strictly speaking, Kristina wasn't sticking to the section they'd staked out, but that shouldn't be a problem. They weren't at war with the other tribes inside Lucky's, but like in high school, it was usually best to stay in your place. On high school's Day One, you found a spot to eat lunch, and it had better be a good one because you were committed and would be eating there for the rest of the year.

At least, that had been high school for Kristina. Nerds ate in the corner by the trashcans, popular kids ate on the main stairwell as a gauntlet for lessers who dared pass that way, burnouts ate between joints outside by the dumpsters, and Kristina ate alone, standing by her locker, because everyone knew her mother was the one who'd lobbied to have the uniform skirts lengthened from Sexy Schoolgirl to Amish Frump.

So it had been in the casino for the past week — everyone in their spot with an unwritten rule not to trespass. Although, with the alien ships finally *present* rather than just *on their way*, that might change.

Kristina gave it six weeks at most until the entire

planet went full Mad Max. Beyond that — and, technically, before that — humanity became savages. Soon they'd all be wearing socks with sandals. As civilization descended into anarchy, everyone would be eating salad with their shrimp forks. Her parents would be aghast enough to suffer heart attacks in tandem. With any luck, they already had.

Still, out of habit, Kristina's hand strayed into her pocket and pulled out a tiny canister of pepper spray. It was almost always there because the days of her carrying a purse were hit and miss. Purses were for girls, and Kristina had always felt above such things.

Girls — *pshaw*. What did *robots* carry? Or dinosaurs. Kristina could really get into being a robot dinosaur instead of joining the ranks of the "girls" she'd known. Like *Lisa*. Or *Joanna*. Not Margaret. That woman was papery like last year's wasp nest. If Margaret had once been a girl, it was only in a technical sense. She talked like a former dancer, but that was nuts because she was built like a tree stump and resembled a scarecrow.

And *these* were supposed to be her models for femininity? It was a poor set of options. Kristina could be a ditz, a dumb ass, or a smoky-throated has-been. Only, that was too much credit. To be a Has-Been, you had to have been a Once-Was. So far, Margaret's best story was of shooting a would-be robber in the ass cheek in order to save her employer's cheap beer and Twinkies.

Kristina found herself at a bay of windows overlooking the patio. There'd been restaurant seating out there when the hotel had been operational rather than this parody of its former self. If she ignored the missing dead maid and the blood spot, the place was nice enough, shaded by tall palms and the neighboring building. They'd erected slat-top porticos to block all but high-noon sun where the light still shone. Vegas was dry, leaving daytime shade comfortable most of the time. There'd probably been many happy memories forged on that patio. Kristina wondered if anyone had been there when the maid jumped to her death. That one would have been a keeper, for sure.

She was still staring at the bloodstain, now absent its stainer. An emotion threatened to bubble up where Kristina didn't want it to. Maybe fear, probably sadness, perhaps a panic-filled downward spiral without any bottom.

Blackness stretching into forever.

Kristina didn't want to see the face of those

emotions, so she did what Mother had taught her over candles and *foie gras*, their own table set with the finest flatware and a maid — no stain for her — making domestic circuits in the background.

She pushed it down and entirely away. Adult Kris could still remember what Young Kris had brought home that day — frantic tears over a group of girls who'd made her feel like garbage.

Mother hadn't been sympathetic. Father had been in the study, playing Bach on the piano. *They called me weird. They called me a freak!*

And Mother had said, *Stop whining. Blubbering solves nothing.*

Then she'd risen from the table and left Kristina to finish her dinner alone.

Mother refused to bid her a goodnight on account of it only encouraging her daughter's moodiness. She was the black sheep. Her sisters never had breakdowns like this, and neither did Wyatt.

Where had Kristina Louise Fine gone so terribly wrong?

"Exciting, isn't it?"

Kristina turned her head too quickly, startled enough that she forgot to affect her typical disinterest, and saw Margaret the Cynic three suite doors down. She half-lidded her wide eyes and turned her mouth into a slit of animate boredom. "What are you talking about?"

"Death."

"Okay. Whatever."

Margaret raised a slim cigarette to her lips and lit it with a cheap plastic lighter. With her lips pursed, words came out muffled. "It must be worse for you, being young."

"But easy for you."

"Easi*er*," Margaret said, exhaling from the corner of her mouth, now holding the lit cigarette between her first two fingers. "You start to see your own death as inevitable, but that doesn't make it easy."

"Keep smoking, then," Kristina said, starting to turn away. "It's good practice."

"Why are you here?" Margaret asked.

"I wanted to take a walk. Everyone downstairs moved from annoying to intolerable."

"I meant, *Why are you here.* In the hotel at all."

"I told you. I had a gig."

"At Lucky's."

"*Yeah* at Lucky's." There was an implication behind Margaret's words, but Kristina couldn't quite see it all. She waited, but the old woman offered no elaboration.

"Why are *you* here?"

Margaret took another puff, leaning on the doorframe like a diva. "I like the slots. They make me feel like I have some control over my life."

"Random machines make you feel like you have control?"

"I've got a whole philosophy." She took another drag. "You'd just make fun of it."

"I actually meant, 'Why are you up *here?*' Don't you want to keep panicking with Abbott and Company, wondering when it will end?"

"I told you. I have my own thoughts on death. I always figured I'd pass in my sleep, probably in a place like this." Margaret looked around as if just noticing the hallway. Seen through those eyes, Lucky's wasn't impressive. "But if it's by aliens, that's okay, too." She looked to the door behind her. "I figured I'd go to bed. Try again in the morning if we're still here. If the aliens haven't eaten us."

"So, you think that thing was an alien," Kristina said.

"I see." Margaret blew a plume of smoke. "You still think it was a dog."

Kristina shrugged. "I can't be sure. Nobody threw a stick for it."

"Why are you like this?"

She scoffed. Kristina wasn't used to being challenged in conversation, and Margaret's abject cool was giving her the upper hand. Maybe she was scared. Maybe seeing that black thing on the patio and the maid's head rolling from its open jaws had been more than ho-hum. Strange as that might seem.

She moved away from the window, headed for the stairwell.

Margaret moved to block her. She had red hair that had to be dyed, large, deep-set eyes, and narrow features beset by wrinkles. Her posture wasn't pushy at all. It was long, relaxed, and somehow superior. Like Kristina's mother.

"You don't like me," Margaret said.

"Don't take it personally. I don't like anyone."

"Why is that?"

"Because people are stupid."

"Yes. I've heard your act. You reminded me of Sam Kinison."

"Then I think you've got me confused with someone else. He was loud and obnoxious. I'm quiet and clever." Kristina could do better —

maybe a dig at Margaret's old-person memory was in order — but it was like someone had tied her verbal hands. After the incident downstairs, she hadn't felt as quick or as biting. She was a defanged cobra, or a pit bull wearing a muzzle. What a drag.

Margaret seemed to realize. She smiled, but only slightly. "When I saw Kinison back in the day, I wondered how much of his performance was an act. Could anyone really go through life that angry, that worked up?" She didn't finish the thought, taking a dramatic puff instead.

Kristina was apparently supposed to fill in the blanks on her own, see how the Kinison observation applied to her. She moved to pass Margaret again.

"Going back downstairs?"

"If you'll let me." Kristina stared, trying to make her eyes as big and staring as Margaret's. But fat chance.

"Why?"

"What business is it of yours?"

"I'll bet you anything someone suggests we all sleep down there together tonight," Margaret said. "Huddle up like dogs, for the illusion of safety. If they do that, will you be—"

"No."

"What if they break in?"

"Who?" Kristina asked. "The aliens?"

Margaret nodded.

"Why would they break in?"

"Fresh meat."

"That wasn't even one of them," Kristina said, and dammit if her voice wasn't two beats from a warble. Had someone slipped her drugs? Nobody slipped Kristina Fine drugs except for Kristina Fine. She was very discerning. Nothing off the street, just high-class downers of the rich. She'd stolen enough from Mother's cabinet a decade ago to still have a not-quite-expired stockpile.

"Then what was it?" Margaret asked.

"Who cares? It wasn't one of *them*. Everyone can worry about looters and rioters and roving rape gangs, and they can fret about the aliens coming out of their big ball bearings and dominating us into sex cults or whatever. Who knows what they do … they probably have three penises and do all the work for you. Maybe it'll be fun. Worry about that big whatever if you want, but it's not related."

"How do you know?"

Kristina looked at her like this was obvious. "Because the aliens look like us. Big, tall, broad …"

"And skin even whiter'n yours?"

As if Margaret should talk. Yes, Kristina had

the complexion of a Smurf's hat, but the old woman had enough sun damage to crumble her face and the infrastructure beneath it. She could clip off all those sagging folds, make the extra skin into wallets, then sell them in the gift shop. "Yeah. I've heard that, too."

"Great," Kristina said. "Good you're informed. Now get out of my way."

Margaret stepped aside.

Kristina looked over, sure she was being patronized. Then she descended the steps. As she walked, she was unnerved by the concrete echo. There was a strange, unwelcome feeling in her gut. Its long arms wanted to reach up and cradle her lungs, not to repress her breath but to make it feel heavy.

Kristina swallowed, and something foreign bobbed in her throat.

Fuck this.

Fuck Margaret.

And fuck everyone in this stupid casino.

Why was she here?

Because she was a goddamn star, that's why. She'd killed the first night for a group of maybe thirty, then murdered again the third night before a group of three times as many. News was spreading about comedy's up-and-comer, and not just online.

It seemed that Vegas itself had gotten the memo. The fifth night she was supposed to start a one-week engagement in LA, upstairs at Cameo surrounded by opportunity. But that's when the announcement that alien ships were approaching hit the planet and ruined everything.

Kristina was undaunted. She'd called Iris and asked how she should get to LA now that flights were grounded, but instead of offering to order a car, she'd yelled something unintelligible and hung up instead. There had been screaming and shouting in the background — Iris herself hadn't sounded professional. She sounded more like a hack, the kind of manager who made things other than her star's best interests a priority.

Kristina had stewed for a while. She'd get a new manager, if Iris planned to be so unreliable. It took twenty-four hours of belligerent thoughts before she decided to act, but the new management firm refused to answer the phone. She took a big risk after that, calling Harvey Biltman even though he wasn't taking new comedians, just to ask for referrals.

Kristina's star was on the rise — even temperamental, rage-prone Harvey knew that. But Harvey Biltman's wife had answered the phone, crying, sobbing and begging Kristina to please not be dead. Only after hanging up did she realize that the wife might have been talking to Harvey. Another lead dead … maybe literally.

So she'd stayed. And she'd planned. And while the others got in a circle to make introductions and discuss their feelings, Kristina kept her distance and worked on her act.

Invasions really did bring out the most amusing qualities in people, putting all of their foibles and scars on display. She had a whole bit on Lisa, though she rearranged the letters to *Ilsa*, and it was an honest-to-God laugh riot. She'd perform it for the pains-in-the-ass downstairs if they'd stop bitching and whining and give her a stage. And leave their emotional baggage at the door.

Thus buoyed, Kristina marched across the dark part of the casino floor. This was technically the convention center tribe's territory, but she had her pepper spray and was ready to pummel the nerds.

She found the group just ten feet from where she'd left them, arriving with a head full of steam but all of a sudden uncertain just what she planned to do with it.

Was she going to explain who she was and how bright her future had so recently been? Was she going to make fun of them one by one, to prove they needn't take things so seriously? She'd even worked up a cutting joke involving the big black toothy creature and the decapitated maid. If they'd stop insisting on being so goddamned solemn for a minute, they might really get a kick out of it.

But they all still looked like beaten puppies. She saw Dennis, the doctor turned Pit Boss, Todd the Armored Car Driver, and the Groom comforting his erstwhile Bride despite her recent decision that he was a piece of shit who deserved to die.

Nobody around here could stick to their guns.

She saw the Gambler, too, but he wouldn't want to play. With Margaret upstairs, that left Has-Been lounge rat Jeremy, the Magician, and of course Lisa the Showgirl with pleading eyes like tide pools. Most people didn't really look like lambs when they were acting sheeplike, but Lisa did. Or maybe she looked like a fuck doll. Or maybe, for the pervs down here, both at once.

"Listen," Kristina said as they all watched her arrive, "we can't just sit on our asses and wait for something to happen. I don't know about any of you, but I've got things to do. I have a job. I—"

At that moment, Lucky's entire front wall exploded.

FOUR

The Twins

JOHN WAS JUST ABOUT to open his mouth to suggest Kristina shut hers when the world turned upside-down. The air filled with debris, litter, and shrapnel, most of which was blocked by rows of one-armed bandits, and although he didn't realize it at first, the enormous blast actually knocked him from sitting to the filthy carpet.

In the few seconds it took to square reality with what had just happened, it seemed to John that he was still upright and a wall of slow-moving detritus was scrolling slowly upward in front of him. Then two facts dawned, bang-bang one after the other. The first was that the detritus wasn't slow at all but his perception of time had been knocked from its rocker as surely as had John himself. The second was that the debris wasn't flying vertically upward. Rather, wreckage was drifting nearly horizontally toward him from the front, and only his supine position distorted his view.

There'd been a moment of supernatural brightness — the kind of glow that comes not from fire or a flashlight or the sun, but from a welder's arc or volatile metals burning at thousands of degrees. If the blast had been longer — or if any of them had kept looking at it, but of course they all flinched away — he'd likely have scorched his retinas.

Instead, the burst lasted only a fractional second, illuminating every cornered nuance of the room like a relief drawing. As soon as it'd come it was gone, and John, after blinking and brushing glass from his face, sat up to see the casino darker than it had been before.

The power must have blown — or more accurately *been* blown by the explosion up front. Even the patio light, where Maria's body had been until recently, was off. The only illumination now was from the crescent moon and the front wall of what used-to-be doors but were now little more than embers and flames.

John heard Lawrence ask Joanna, "Are you okay?" in a tone of voice that was only tender.

Then he heard Joanna's response — a shove, a tussle, and the straightening of both body and clothes.

John felt a drip on his cheek. He raised a finger, touched the wet spot, then held up the finger in the flickering orange light to see darkness there. He winced at the blood, wondering about the width of the gash on his cheek.

Quick recon said he was otherwise whole, and a glance at the others said they were either unhurt or barely injured.

There was shouting through the chaos. But John's own group behind him wasn't the source. They were mumbling and asking small questions but not yet panicked.

The shouts were coming from ahead and to the left. From another tribe.

John rushed forward, dodging machines that were decreasingly whole and undamaged the closer he came to the fire's source. He saw an almost comical level of devastation upon arrival. In a ten-yard semicircle beyond the blown-out doors, everything that could possibly fall had rained in a starburst. A few of the slots up front looked almost melted, and the members so recently holding the glass doors were warped beyond recognition. The air was hot, and not just from the flames.

But that wasn't what drew his attention most.

The thing burning his eyes was overwhelming to see at first. He almost wanted to gaze at it sideways and force the sight into sense.

A commotion stopped him.

John turned to the enormous oddity, unable to assimilate its presence but unwilling to let it entirely out of his view.

Across the now gaping entrance, a small clot of others were staring with open mouths.

"What … What is it?" asked a man at the front of the new group. "What just happened?"

The confused man was replaced almost immediately by two others. A black-haired guy and a black-haired gal, both thirty-ish and wielding shotguns.

The man raised his, pointing alternately at John and the massive object now inside the Lucky's lobby.

John raised his hands. "Whoa! Whoa, whoa!"

A clicking sound came from his left.

John looked over, surprised to see Margaret holding a gun that could've given Dirty Harry an inferiority complex. A few days ago she'd announced that she never left the house without protection, but that proclamation had seemed directed at Jeremy, who was about her age, so John gave 50/50 odds that she'd been talking about condoms. The other half of his supposition centered on something discreet and fitting of her age. A pearl-handled pistol, perhaps, ideally an antique thing with two triggers and two two-inch barrels. But this cannon was bigger than both of her hands put together, and she was holding it — and he had to admire how *steadily* — on the two newcomers with shotguns.

"Okay." John patted the air in a gesture of peace. "Let's all just settle down. How about we lower our weapons?"

"Bullshit!" said the dark-haired man. His eyes showed white all around the iris.

"We're all friends here," John said.

"We're not your friends! You're that crew from the main floor!"

"We're not a crew," John said in his most soothing voice. "We're just people. People like you, who got stuck here. All we want is shelter, same as you." He waited, unsure of what to expect. They all knew there were several non-overlapping groups inside Lucky's, but until now, that had been an academic understanding.

The dark-haired woman said, "I know you, too. You're the ones who have the restaurant."

"That's not us. That's—"

"*The patio restaurant!*" she spat. "The one with the food stores!"

"Calm down." John was still patting the air. "We never meant to hoard the food. You're welcome to whatever you need."

"Well …" said Lawrence from behind him.

Margaret was more direct, still with her hand cannon raised and rock-steady. "Get your own fucking food."

The woman swung her shotgun toward Margaret.

John moved to intercept.

He was bold enough to go toward the converging weapons but not stupid enough to actually get between them. He raised his hands again, now with one to each side, one for Margaret and one for the others. "Okay! Okay. Just … It's fine. One problem at a time, what'dya say?"

That bit of non-logic must have made sense, or else it tricked Margaret and the others into thinking it *should*. Guns lowered by inches.

"We need to talk," said the man. "This it isn't over."

Several of the group — six or seven people, from what John could see — murmured agreement. The man lowered his weapon, but the woman looked at Margaret with her own still raised, aimed somewhere roughly between her and John, and the enormous object the room had yet to acknowledge.

John pointed. The thing was probably twelve feet tall and wouldn't have fit on any of the floors above, given headspace here only because the casino was double-high. A perfect sphere and, by all appearances, entirely unmarred by whatever had happened. A small panel at the lower front closed before John could register that it had been open, and a small nozzle-like thing vanished like a blink.

Maybe the silver sphere itself hadn't exploded. That would explain the total lack of damage. Maybe it had *blown* a hole in the hotel, then flown into that aperture before coming to rest.

But why?

"Margaret." John gave her a nod then turned to the woman. "What's your name?"

"Olivia," she said grudgingly.

He put a hand on his chest. "I'm John. It's nice to meet you. And you are …?"

He waited. The black-haired man didn't answer, so eventually the woman said, "This is my twin brother Taylor."

"Okay. Margaret. Taylor. Olivia. We ended up in different parts of the hotel, but a week ago we were all just people. I might have sat at the bar with you and had a drink. Forget 'crews.' We're all human." He had to throw the dice, seeing as they still seemed unconvinced. "And there's something outside — something that can now walk right in." He moved one arm to indicate their new western exposure. "So, I don't know about you all, but I'm going to put my weapon down" — John noticed, belatedly, that he'd picked up a length of pipe and likely looked more antagonistic than he'd realized — "and just talk like people. What'dya say?"

"Her first," said the man.

John nodded at Margaret.

"What if he shoots me?" Margaret said to nobody in particular.

"He won't," said Todd.

Because he drove an armored car, and possibly because cops never really stopped being cops, Todd also carried a gun. After it became apparent that they were all stuck together, he'd changed into civilian clothes and moved the weapon from a holster to the back of his pants. He still carried it everywhere, but for once in their short relationship, John and Todd were on the same wavelength.

Margaret, maybe because she was remembering the same thing or because they couldn't stay in a standoff forever, lowered her weapon and, taking her time, flipped on the safety then returned the gun to her purse.

The man followed suit, going so far as to hand his shotgun to one of the others behind him. Realizing she was the only armed one left, Olivia did the same.

"So now we're all friends," said Dennis.

"What's that mean?" asked one of the others.

"*Nothing,*" John said. "It means nothing … right, Dennis. We're through here. Through being tough and fighting among our own species. Agreed?"

Nods circled the congregation.

John, deciding fewer people was better, waved his group back — all but Margaret, the constant Cynic, who wasn't prepared to trust anyone.

Seeing this, Olivia waved her own crew back, including those holding the shotguns. She muttered something that sounded like, "tell the others and stay there," then looked at Taylor. He finally softened from his high alert.

When just the four of them were alone, John nodded at the twins a silent question — *We good here?*

Olivia nodded back.

All eyes turned to the alien craft. In the time John had spent looking away from it, he'd decided his assessment that it was unmarred must be wrong. He just hadn't looked closely enough. Of course the craft would have scratches and warps caused by white-hot flame. At the very least, the thing would be sullied with soot from the fire.

But now that they were all looking closely, John saw none of those things. Not a single scratch or speck of dirt. No soot. Even the machine surfaces were perfect. The edges were completely invisible. If not for seeing that little nozzle door close, he wouldn't believe it was there.

A perfect sphere of stainless steel. Its presence amid the destruction and still-burning fires was a contradiction.

The sight was impossible.

"What the hell is it?" Taylor said.

"It's one of their ships," Margaret replied.

John was mentally measuring dimensions. It was without question an alien ship — one of the smaller ones the news called a "shuttle." But the creature they'd seen an hour ago was too big and too long for this thing.

That was comforting in a way. It lended unreal credence to the idea that what they'd seen, despite all evidence, was not an alien being. He was obviously deceiving himself — the biggest dogs and tigers in the world didn't have ten rows of teeth or blue sparks churning inside their bellies. But now that they were seeing the shuttle plain as day, he could conclude that whatever was inside — if there *was* anything — wasn't that kind of creature.

John thought of the news reports and pirate radio broadcasts, claiming to have seen beings emerging from ships or just, as rumors, walking free. They were supposed to be powder-white, humanoid but larger, bland in manner and imposing in stature. "Invasion of the Body Builders," one wiseacre had joked, but the mental hook was a useful one. After hearing it, John knew he'd always have a framework for whatever else he'd eventually see.

Taylor moved closer to it.

John said, "Careful," as if it might be worthy of utterance.

Soon all four of them were circling the craft.

After a minute or so, Olivia reached out to touch it.

He almost said "careful" again, but this time he kept his mouth shut. Who was he to preach caution? He'd been planning to blow his own head off a week ago. With so little future and so many guns, maybe he still would.

"It's cold," Olivia said.

John reached out and laid his palm flat on the metal — or what looked like metal. The surface was like a heat sink, stealing heat from his hand. He yanked it away, and it took several minutes before warmth returned.

"What do we do now?" Margaret asked.

The sphere answered for her.

There was a hiss and a click, then everyone jumped back.

Three long black lines appeared as if from nowhere on the side, quickly joining to form three-fourths of an upright rectangle. White gas, or steam, spewed from the seams. A fourth side of the rectangle appeared, then the smooth silver metal in the center seemed to fade away.

John forced himself to breathe.

He couldn't peel his eyes from what could only

be a doorway, but he could see the twins to one side, equally frozen.

The space wasn't just dark, indicating a lack of light. It was, instead, tangible blackness like a strip of pure black velvet.

But then something emerged.

A bright white island rising from that ochre sea.

The black around the white thing rippled as if the blackness were liquid.

The island of white grew larger. Became a massive hand. A massive arm.

Then whatever was inside gave out, and the arm's slow egress gave way to something more all-at-once.

"Holy shit," said John, looking at the big powder-white alien — unconscious, dead, he had no idea — lying on the patterned casino carpet among all the damage.

Olivia was at his left hip.

"You can say that again," she said.

FIVE

The Magician

LAWRENCE WAS STRIKING OUT.

For a while there, he thought all the danger and drama — a creature outside, bickering within the group, reminders that the aliens hadn't yet shown themselves to the wider media and hence might be up to anything — would cause Joanna to retreat into the safety of the one person here she actually knew. And for a little while it had worked.

After the nightmare outside had bared its teeth, shown that unnatural spark, and belted its cry, he and Joanna had huddled together for mutual soothing. The spell broke soon after, and Joanna remembered she was pissed at him, but in truth Lawrence was ready to knock it off anyway.

He did want her back, but he'd grown increasingly sure that his attempts at courting and apology were making him look like a stalker. It wasn't that way, though. They'd been friends forever. His love, for the few moments she'd returned it, had been genuine and good. The kind of thing the world needed more of right now. But somewhere he'd gone wrong, and he'd done the wrong thing — or at the very least, he *looked* like he was doing the wrong thing to literally everyone but himself.

Now, he was catching eyes from everyone. Especially that hardass, Kristina. According to an impromptu routine she'd done this morning after Joanna's first rant, Lawrence had practically assaulted her.

But he wasn't that guy. It wasn't like that at all.

To prove it, he tried giving Joanna space.

Then Joanna came to him with one petty excuse after another, sniping at him while he minded his own business. To test things — and also to allow what she claimed to so desperately want — he'd even gone to Dennis and asked if he had the power to perform divorces as well.

He couldn't do *divorces*, but Dennis could do *annulments*, and he'd delivered the info to Joanna the next time she dropped by to yell at him.

Fine, I misunderstood. We both decided to get married,

but you say I pushed things. The security footage, which must be somewhere, would show us both laughing, but okay, I'm the bad guy.

He wasn't even being facetious. His long-standing desire to please her became remorse even though he didn't think he'd done wrong.

So, I'll fix it. I'll split us up. Dennis says he can do it. Let's do it right now.

But somehow that had made her even angrier. To Lawrence, it seemed like he'd called her bluff — who wanted *more* separation from people right now? — but Joanna had spouted something about coercion and gaslighting and him being a manipulative shit she'd never seen coming, but still she kept coming around. On the bright side, Kristina had seen it all and started making fun of Joanna after that. He supposed it was a victory. Or whatever.

He pushed his luck, trying to be kind but getting sneered at as a result. Whether others thought he was a creep or not, Lawrence resolved to keep trying. He wouldn't push her to breaking, and he'd try not to get her alone so the group could act as their mutual arbiter. But he also wouldn't shy away from looking like an asshole one last time. She was still his closest friend. Too much had transpired between them to just let it go.

He pulled her aside in full view of Jeremy, the singer, and Amerigo, who did magic or something.

"I just want to talk," he said.

"Why, so you can trick me again?"

He'd been ready for that. As many times as she'd used that single line, it'd lost all its punch. "That's not a sensible response. I'm here and you're here, in this place with people around. We're sitting in chairs, sober. How exactly am I going to trick you?"

"Oh, piss off, Lawrence."

He waited for her to leave. She didn't. So he did.

She called after him. "I see. Stalking off and pouting again?"

"What exactly do you want me to do here? Do you want me to stay?"

"I'm not your boss. Do whatever the hell you want."

"Fine. I'm going to leave."

"You aren't winning, you know," she said, crossing her legs and turning her torso sideways, away from him. "Don't start thinking that you're leaving me all defeated."

"That doesn't even make sense!"

Jeremy stood, trying to see toward the front

where the giant sphere had crashed. They'd been sent away to lessen the feeling of confrontation with the other group, but unspoken mutual consent had kept them from going all the way back toward the restaurant and the windows through which they'd seen the monster. They were somewhere new, surrounded by slots taller than Lawrence.

"I can't see anything," Jeremy said. "I'm going to sneak back."

"Don't do that." Kristina sounded uncharacteristically serious. "Those bitches with the shotguns looked pretty unstable."

"One was a man," Lawrence said, looking over.

"*Bitch* is a unisex term nowadays, you misogynist bitch."

Lawrence wasn't sure what to make of that. He looked at Joanna, but she'd rotated even further away. It was a passive aggressive move, simultaneously asking for his attention and demanding that he leave her alone.

Maybe he should. He was good guy.

He held doors for people and gave to charity and coached his nephew's soccer team once he lost the weight and started feeling active.

He volunteered at the food pantry and turned

his work in on time and paid compliments and never complained behind people's backs.

He seldom drank, last night being a notable exception, didn't use drugs or stay up late. He kept his house clean.

His self esteem had taken a hit as a kid, but if he'd bothered to rethink the whole issue from zero, now he realized he'd felt good about himself for a long time — years and years.

Only in the Joanna sector of his life did he feel like a loser — first because he'd been one when they met, then because she dated idiots and that seemed to mean that he, by comparison, was worse than an idiot because she had zero interest in him. He felt bad for pining and worse for his adoration going unrequited. Now he felt guilty because she thought he'd duped her and deflated by her rejection.

Something about the relationship wasn't working, and not just for her. So maybe *holding on* was the problem. Maybe if he let their blowout stand and simply waited until it was over to pick up the pieces, that might be better.

Let her hate him. Maybe it was for the best.

"What's it mean, do you think?" The voice was so small, at first Lawrence didn't realize it was talking to him. Especially considering it came from someone who had sworn off of talking to him.

"Are you talking to me now?" he asked.

"I'm sorry. I'm just upset."

"I didn't mean to fool you. I thought we both—"

"I'm not talking about that," she snapped — a bit of Angry Joanna returning to say her piece. "We'll talk about *that* later."

He exhaled. So this was how it was going to be. She wanted to partition one self from the other. One part of her was furious at him and the other needed his help, his friendship. His instinct was right — this just wasn't worth it. He could find some other woman to obsess about. Right now, seeing how bad it could be, Lawrence wanted his friend back.

He'd brought up the annulment with venom. This time he meant it.

"Look. Let's just end it. It's fine. I swear. I didn't mean to do anything you didn't want, so okay, it was my mistake. Let's talk to Dennis. We can just go back to the way things were."

"Lawrence …"

"I'm serious. It's for the best." And, taking a chance, he reached for her hand.

She took it, surprising him. Then she let him pull her upright.

They had to search a bit to find Dennis but eventually found him fiddling with a slot machine that must have had a battery or something, because unlike the rest of their area — lit now by the fire up front, moon glow in back, and the flashlight from someone's soon to be dead phone — that one machine had power.

But he wasn't pulling levers or pushing buttons. He was messing with some sort of control panel toward the bottom.

"Dennis, we—" Lawrence said.

"You know, it's funny. I used to see these stupid clickbait ads online all the time. They had headlines like, 'Casinos hate this but they can't stop you.' It always looked like people were using special rings to somehow beat the odds. Like James Bond did. Or someone in one of those movies. I just remember a magnetic ring that made slot machines hit."

"I think that was Q," Lawrence said.

Dennis sighed. He wasn't really listening, despite his talking. He turned to the front, toward where the corner of that huge steel ball could still be seen.

"I couldn't take medical school. I made myself

finish, but then I couldn't take being a doctor. I had a friend who worked here, and somehow I ended up a Vegas pit boss. How did that happen? I used to think my life belonged to me."

"Dennis, Lawrence says you can—"

"You just end up on autopilot," Dennis continued, cutting Joanna off. "Things happen, and only afterward do you stop to wonder why or how. Like the magnetic ring that lets you win at slot machines. It's controlling things, but everyone assumes it's fate. Or luck."

"I don't think magnets would work on modern slot machines," Lawrence said, splitting hairs and missing the point. "Anyway …"

Dennis looked them both over. "So, you want to do it, huh?"

Lawrence nodded.

"You know last night's papers didn't get filed, right? I just went through the motions. Your license is in a pile of stuff that'll be sent out if there's ever mail again, but I've gotta say I have my doubts. Did you know there's a mothership over Moscow, and the Russians are talking about shooting nukes at it? They do that — we do that — and it's all over." He shook himself as if dismissing a trance. "Anyway.

Point is, we don't really need to jump through hoops. I can just tear up—"

A strange noise came from the next row of slots. From where the cell phone flashlight shone.

"What was that?" Joanna asked.

They moved back to where they'd been just in time to see Amerigo Cross with his head tilted back, eyes rolled up to the whites. His mouth was open, and a monastic hum was reverberating from deep in his lungs. He was dressed entirely in black like always, his superbly coiffed hair an unshakable mass atop his pretty head. With his back arched so severely, his blazer's rear hung below him like a poor man's cape.

Dennis looked at Todd. They'd bonded because both had given up promising careers to do something less impressive.

"Is this some sort of magic trick?" Dennis asked. Then to Cross, he said, "Hey! Amerigo! Is this a magic trick?"

"Don't ask him that," Todd said. "I'm tired of his mystical bullshit about how magic is real."

Dennis looked worried. "I don't think this is bullshit."

Lawrence moved closer. Cross was drooling a

little, his eyes still rolled all the way up, still fully white. He whispered, *"Amerigo. Are you okay?"*

No answer.

"You can tell me. I won't blow your illusion."

No answer.

"You're kind of freaking us out."

He responded without words, his eyes glowing blue. His hands clenched and unclenched as if trying to grasp an unknown something. He appeared to spiral down inside a very particular kind of pain. The kind that bunched muscles into knots.

It looked like the man was being electrocuted.

He staggered, fell to the ground, then began to jig and kick.

Shouts — John, Margaret, the new people — came from the front door. Lawrence was torn. Cross's problem was right in front of them, but John's shouts sounded more like alarm than pain. Whereas Amerigo Cross might be dying, John's yell made it sound like soon, if someone didn't act, they'd *all* be dying.

"What's going on?" Todd demanded of nobody in particular, standing.

Kristina ran toward the front doors, despite her earlier misgivings.

Joanna knelt. So did Lawrence.

Cross was gone, replaced by this helpless wretch before them.

"He's having a seizure," Lawrence said. "What do you do for a seizure?"

"Stick something in his mouth," Todd suggested. "We have to clear his airway."

"Don't put anything in his mouth!" Dennis cried out, rushing over.

"What about a pencil to bite on?" Joanna sounded panicked. "So he doesn't bite off is tongue?"

It was moot. Cross's mouth looked like the entrance to a cave.

"Roll him onto his side," said Joanna. "So he doesn't choke on his puke."

Jeremy entered the scene. "He's not puking."

"Roll him onto his side, anyway!"

Lawrence was reaching when Dennis held up a hand. "Wait. It's stopping."

The seizure sputtered and died. Then Amerigo was still.

Todd said, "Is he dead? Tell me he's not dead."

Dennis shook his head. "He's not dead."

Jeremy shrugged. "Maybe we should roll him like you said. He looks like he could puke now."

Joanna put her face in her hands. She leaned against Lawrence, who found himself simultaneously scared and confused.

"Wait," Dennis said. "What's this?" His fingers were in Cross's mouth, and Lawrence could only think of the seizure. If someone could bite off their own tongue, what's to say his fingers weren't next?

Dennis pulled something out, holding it between his index and middle fingers. A small thing, slippery, round, and silver. He was having a hard time not dropping it back down Amerigo's throat.

He put it on the carpet. They all looked at it.

Amerigo remained still.

"Is that ..." Todd squinted. "It looks like a BB!"

"It's too small to be a BB."

"A ball bearing, then."

Without warning, Amerigo sat up. The move looked impossible, according to the laws of physics, because he didn't seem to use a single limb to assist him.

"Oh my God," said Dennis.

The tiny BB thing was floating above Amerigo's head. It had risen in perfect time with the magician himself, as if its motion had pulled him into place. Now it hovered unsupported. Tiny, perfectly round, and flawlessly smooth. The same burnished alloy as the twelve-foot shuttle up front.

The shouting up there had stopped as well.

They were all staring at Amerigo, who still hadn't moved from his board-stiff sitting position. Amerigo had his eyes back, but they looked vacant, like a man deep in a spell of hypnosis.

Kristina rushed back into the circle. "Guys! Something came out of that ship up front. An alien. And right now, it just … *holy fuck.*"

She'd spied Amerigo. Felt for a chair. Dropped into it.

"W-what's going on up front?" Lawrence asked.

The voice that came from Amerigo's throat belonged to someone or something else. Deeper, dropped by bass modulation.

"This body is damaged. Do not touch it, and it will be retrieved. There will be consequences if the body is moved."

"We touched him," Joanna said. "Oh, shit. We touched him!"

"Clear the area for retrieval. Do not attempt to leave. The city is being monitored. A gate has been established that you cannot pass. End."

"*Gate?*" Jeremy repeated.

"*End?*" Dennis asked.

Amerigo spoke again. "This body is damaged. Do not touch it, and it will be retrieved. There will be consequences if the body is moved. Clear the area for retrieval. Do not attempt to leave. The city is being monitored. A gate has been established that you cannot pass. End."

Lawrence said, "It's a message. Someone write it down."

Dennis fumbled in his pocket, but the tiny silver ball shot so fast toward the front that it might have blipped from existence before he could procure anything.

Another gasp and chatter from the front door, then all was silent.

Amerigo had already collapsed. He was on his back again, head sideways, chest slowly rising and falling.

"What just happened?" Jeremy ran a hand through his smart white hair. "Was he …? Is he …?"

Dennis had fingers to Amerigo's neck. "He's alive. Pulse is steady." More checks. "I think he's just asleep."

"*Asleep?*" Lawrence said.

"How?" Joanna asked.

Dennis lightly slapped his cheeks. "Amerigo. Hey Amerigo. You okay?"

Lawrence looked toward Kristina. "What's going on up there? What did you say about an alien?"

Jeremy had pulled a small notepad from his inner pocket and was writing deliberately with a ballpoint pen, mouthing words as he went. *"Do not … attempt … to leave. The city is …"* He looked up. "Something about a gate?"

"What's going on?" Amerigo asked, now on his feet. Nobody had seen him stand.

"Amerigo!" Dennis turned back after having just looked away, his expression and voice both full of relief.

"You're okay?" Joanna asked.

"Yeah, I'm fine." He paused then said, "Why are you all staring at me?"

"GET UP HERE!" The voice was a sudden bellow, coming from the front.

Everyone looked at each other, then the visible crescent of silver sphere, before rushing forward.

Kristina, finally without her cool, pointed at the huge white object. A few of the new ones shrieked and everyone stepped back as if the thing might infect them.

"It was mouthing words," Kristina said to Joanna, Lawrence, Dennis, Todd, Jeremy, and Amerigo." Then she looked at John, Margaret, and the black-haired twins. "And he" — she pointed at Amerigo — "he was … I think he was saying the words the alien was mouthing!"

"How?" John asked.

"*Why?*" asked Taylor, the male twin.

Words came too fast. Following who said what was like tracking a ball in a BINGO hopper.

"Maybe they don't talk. The aliens. Maybe they can't make sounds."

"What are you saying? That *he* was talking for it?"

"It sounded like a recorded message," said Dennis. "You all heard it."

"*We* didn't hear it," countered John.

Jeremy had his notebook out, reading. "'This body is broken.' 'Don't touch it.' 'We'll retrieve it.' Something about consequences."

"What consequences?" Olivia asked. "For what?"

"Wait. They're going to *retrieve the body?*"

"Don't you guys think we should be focusing on that thing about *consequences?*"

"Then that thing about not leaving the city," Jeremy kept going. "*The city is watched.*"

"Monitored," Dennis corrected.

"The city is monitored. There's a gate you can't go through.'

John said, "Slow down, I don't get what you're saying."

So Dennis described what had happened from start to end, and afterward Margaret explained what Kristina more or less already had — the powder-white alien hadn't risen, but its mouth had said something without saying anything, all right.

"Here," said Kristina, shoving her phone into the huddle's center. "I'll prove it."

Then she navigated to her camera roll and played a video she must have taken when the others weren't paying attention to her. The screen showed the alien's hairless white face, humanlike eyes closed, its mouth moving.

"Same words." Dennis nodded. "It used Amerigo like a puppet."

"What?" Amerigo said.

"Oh, be happy," said Kristina, pocketing her phone. "You're finally as creepy as you've always wanted to be.

"It was that ball thing," said Todd.

"Yes! The ball thing." Lawrence described it for the others.

"So that's what that was," said John, thinking. "What?"

"Something zoomed over here from where you were. It hit the ship and made the metal … well, it sort of rippled like throwing a pebble into a pond. Whatever came over here was about the size you described."

It seemed that all cards were now on the table, but still nothing made sense. A curious sensation, knowing everything yet understanding nothing.

Jeremy was still thumbing through his little notebook. Lawrence didn't have a photographic memory, but from what he heard, the old man had gotten things just about right: a repeating message for all of them, delivered through the mouth of another human being.

For them.

Lawrence felt a chill. It hadn't dawned on him, in all the confusion, that those words hadn't merely happened. On the contrary. They'd been directed, meant specifically for those inside.

Was it the alien before them who'd spoken?

Or something else, from somewhere else?

"*There's a gate*," Jeremy read, "*that you cannot pass.*"

They all looked to John, their default leader.

The twins — leaders of the other group — looked only at each other.

"'A gate you cannot pass," John said. "What's that mean? "How are we supposed to know what that means?"

Lisa, who Lawrence hadn't realized was missing until exactly this moment, stood at one end of the circle in a flowered sundress and sandals as if waiting on spring.

"I know what it means," she said. "Ask me."

The Showgirl

Lisa didn't understand what happened.

One moment she was down in the casino with the others while Kristina, who definitely seemed to hate her, ranted about this or that yet again. The next moment — just as she heard something explosive, distant and suffocated by mountains of cotton wadding — Lisa found herself alone in the desert.

It was dark outside, but she was able to easily see around in the moonlight. Better than usual, in fact, as if she wasn't using her own eyes.

She was standing beside her father.

"You came to this city of sin, and now God has come to claim the sinners."

He was holding his Bible. He'd never hit Lisa with it before, but he'd done so plenty with both of her brothers. He'd also never put Lisa on his lap and touched her in questionable ways, but five years ago there had been a parabolic dip in their congregation's morale. It plunged when Mr. Trattoria was accused of fondling girls in the daycare and then rose when everyone in the church spontaneously and inexplicably forgot it and never mentioned that little tidbit again.

Lisa remembered it clearly. She'd already gone off to college by then, and because it was a good Christian college, her parents still felt she was going to Heaven. She wanted to dance and act, and that was a lot less acceptable ... but again, thanks to it being a good Christian college, the only dancing was square and the only acting opportunities were in the Nativity play.

Her parents both still believed they could eventually lead Tempted Lisa into the light back then, and in a lot of ways they had. It was the incident with the daycare kids that shook ... well, not her faith. Lisa never lost that.

But she did lose something in the way she looked at her parents, or viewed their infallibility. Lisa did love them both, she supposed, but that love became conditional after the day she found her father on his knees in front of the study's Virgin Mary, begging Her forgiveness.

It wasn't the begging or the plea that bothered her. It was the confirmation that he'd done something that required forgiveness. She knew the affected children. She'd taught them how to braid hair and make friendship bracelets.

They never looked at Lisa the same after that — and she, unlike her father, had done nothing wrong.

"I'm not a sinner, Daddy."

The desert should have felt unreal. It probably was. The place had the texture of a dream. Her father's presence didn't surprise her, and that right there should have given things away. They hadn't spoken in four years, but that wasn't Lisa's doing.

She had tried, and eventually succeeded, in forcing herself to see her father as weak rather than evil — as a man with good intentions but brittle resolve. Her mother, in turn, was devoted, not an accessory — because Mommy knew. Of course she knew. She knew and forgave without condition because that was what her Lord commanded. Lisa, by her own conditional forgiveness, became the larger sinner.

In the end, it wasn't Lisa who kept the family apart. She'd held no grudges and, despite the shame, vowed to say nothing so long as there were no signs that Daddy was at it again. Her parents held the grudge. Her parents blamed Lisa for her sins even though they'd forgiven Daddy for his.

She'd wanted to dance. To act. To be onstage.

Mommy said it was vain, and vanity was a sin — not to mention all the skin and salaciousness she'd ended up showing.

There was a day she would have been cowed by her parents' insistence that she stay home, stay chaste, and do the Lord's work, but that day disappeared when Lisa found her father begging to rid him of longing for little children. She stood by him but, when the time came to decide, stood away from him as well. Her passions were her own, and given her father's personal fires, she decided in the end that she'd never take their views over her own. Not ever again.

"They're all sinners." He brandished the Bible with both hands as if to show it off. "Otherwise, why the pillars of salt?"

Lisa looked. All doubt that she was in a dream

— or, more likely, some sort of fugue state — vanished when she saw a stylized version of Vegas instead of the real thing looming behind her. This was Vegas as her parents imagined it, though they'd never truly seen the place. Nothing but neon and pornographic language. Posters of nude breasts — though those, too, were stylized, as her father's impression of salacious was closer to Lisa's most conservative onstage costumes — and rolling dice.

The Strip was the lone occupant of this imaginary Vegas. There were no homes, and the only businesses were those bound for Hell.

Around this bastardized Vegas, at regular intervals, were tall pillars of salt. Lot's wife, over and over again.

"Daddy, why are you …?"

But he was gone, leaving behind only an arid breeze and a stirring of desert dust.

Lisa looked down. She was wearing black leather lingerie, the kind of thing she'd never worn before and — this always blew her customers' minds — never would. The costumes Lisa wore onstage never actually revealed her breasts or crotch. They came close, but most of what audiences saw was illusion and fantasy. She didn't freelance like many of the other girls, tricking for cash on the side. Lisa was the opposite of promiscuous in her private life. She'd had sex exactly once, with a very handsome man who'd been more awkward than smooth, and in retrospect, she'd felt sorry for him. She hadn't enjoyed it much, mostly because of the guilt. And feeling watched by the Lord.

A silver cross dangled above her leather bra.

She should be cold out here. She was not.

Lisa approached one of the pillars. She heard it whisper.

This body is damaged.

She looked down at her half-exposed breasts. It was the kind of thing her father would say of her career, so she wasn't exactly surprised.

Do not touch it, and it will be retrieved.

Retrieved by whom?

But she did touch it, That was one of her sinful indulgences. One she'd never admit.

The pillar's words became stranger, harder to believe they were meant for her after all.

There will be consequences if the body is moved. Clear the area for retrieval.

Aloud, echoing as if in a very large warehouse, she said, "What?"

Do not attempt to leave. The city is being monitored.

Lisa had been pressing her ear to the pillar. Now she pulled back, wondering.

It was no longer a pillar. In its place was an enormous rock, standing upright on one end. Ten feet away, there was another. And another ten feet after that. The line of stones extended as far as Lisa could see. Each end of the line curved as if bending toward the city's embrace. True Vegas, instead of one borne from her parents' perception.

The sand was cooler beneath her feet. Everything was.

Lisa shivered and realized that she wasn't wearing that black lingerie after all. She was, instead, wearing her flower-patterned sundress and her cutest brown sandals — the ones with just enough heel to move her from short to middle-height.

But heeled sandals were poor footwear in the sand, so she took a step onto concrete. Looking back, she saw concrete behind her as well. The desert was far away. Beyond this line of upright stones.

The rocks whispered again in her mind. *A gate has been established that you cannot pass. End.*

The sky was suddenly darker, though she could still see by the moon and a few buildings clinging to

91

their power. The acrid scent of angry fire filled the air. It was less prominent, with the biggest flames doused days ago, but the burned-rubber, charred-wood reek still assaulted her nostrils.

"A gate?"

A gate.

She looked at the stone monoliths.

Now that reality had resolved, she saw that they hadn't been dropped into the sand as if from above. They'd fallen through inches-thick rebar-reinforced concrete from above. In a few places she could see, homes or shops stood in the way of a boulder's rightful place, but that hadn't stopped the stones. The rocks were twice her height and probably more, surely wider than her wingspan. They must weigh tons.

Not a gate so much as a barrier.

You may walk through them, said an interior voice. *The first time with impunity. The second time will not be so easy.*

Lisa felt stupid speaking aloud, now that the dream state had gone. So she thought her words instead, feeling only slightly less stupid.

All sense of unreality had departed, along with any mental fog. The lightness she'd felt when she'd woken out here — that sense of going along for the ride because nothing made sense in dreams, or perhaps everything did — had disappeared as well.

Now she was just a foolish little girl out on the mean streets of post-invasion Vegas, possibly blocks from gangs they'd heard from Lucky's — packs of human animals who'd like nothing better than to jack her up and strip her for parts.

But Lisa spoke inside herself anyway. Not too different from prayer, and she did that all the time.

Are you real? she asked.

I will be.

What does that mean?

Now is then. Then is now. You are not able to comprehend, so do not try.

Am I really here?

Look around. You will see.

Am I safe?

From us. From me. The rest I cannot say.

How did you bring me here?

You brought you here.

Should I go back to Lucky's?

Should you go back?

She was possessed by an impossible urge to step between the line of rocks, even though she also felt certain that doing so was inadvisable.

The voice had told her she was safe. That she could pass.

So she did, and her mind came alive again.

She saw a thousand life events pass her by like a marching army, flooding her system in less than a second.

Age five, spilling water and breaking Mommy's favorite mug.

Age fourteen and accepting Chris Robie's kiss because it mattered to him if not to her.

Age twenty and stomping to the edge of her school's biomedical sciences building, which was fifteen floors high with only concrete for a landing. Lisa hadn't wanted to jump, but she had been morbidly curious about her own mortality. She remembered wondering about the afterlife. Wondering what it would feel like as she fell, as the cool wind ripped at her clothing as if working to free the fabric from her body. If the arousal of that thought made her a sinner.

Then it all cleared and Lisa was on the other side of the line, looking back at it as if the rocks had attacked her.

You are on your own now, said the voice inside Lisa — the voice, she was sure, that had somehow plucked her from the casino and taken her outside the line of monoliths, to live for moments inside an impressionist's dream.

Desperate not to lose its guidance, Lisa said the most meaningless thing.

I don't know what to call you.

Call me nothing, it said, *because we'll never meet.*

I still want to know.

Then, it said, *call me Stranger.*

And the voice was gone for good.

THE REST of her trip wasn't mystical at all. Just one block later, Lisa decided she'd imagined everything. Only two kinds of people heard voices when nobody was around: crazy people and those touched by God … who, Lisa had decided after visiting parishioners having visions, were crazy too. She wasn't struck by religious mania — she'd never once seen Jesus in a stain, a rag, or a tortilla — and she hadn't, before now, been crazy. Precedent was in her favor.

She'd simply been susceptible, on account of her fatigue. She'd fallen asleep at a strange time, one she was somehow sure had been marked by a tumultuous event she could practically see like a photograph behind her eyelids.

After falling asleep, she had somehow somnambulated for several miles.

The rest could be explained by dream logic.

And the stones? Well, there were definitely stones. She was in the real world now — it was far too shivery cold not to be — and every time she peeked down the avenues toward the outskirts, Lisa could see those giant rocks.

But that wasn't her fault. Aliens could have placed the boulders. She'd just had the bad luck to sleepwalk out to them while the others were …

Well, that issue of the others was definitely a problem.

Lisa wore a delicate silver watch given to her by a lovestruck gambler, and she'd looked at it just as that cranky brunette walked back into their midst. Only about ten minutes had passed. That wasn't enough time to walk all the way out here, let alone have a little chat with Daddy.

Had she been teleported? Her watch hadn't been running slow before tonight.

Her sundress and sandals were also a problem, since she'd been wearing jeans and a tee. She didn't know what the time or the clothes things meant, other than they were weirdnesses she couldn't explain.

Lisa made her way back to find Lucky's front smashed in by what looked like a titanic golf ball. One of those alien shuttles they'd seen hovering in the sky.

There was what appeared to be a dead alien on the ground amid all that smashed glass. Lisa was inoculated against it. After what she'd seen, the situation at Lucky's was noteworthy — but hardly impossible to believe.

The others didn't see her arrive.

She moved behind them, making no effort to stay quiet and attracting zero attention anyway. They were all listening to John, Amerigo the Magician, and Miss No-Fun herself, Kristina the Jokester.

Everyone was talking over each other, working hard to compare notes — to make sense of two distinct happenings she seemed to have missed.

"*A gate you cannot pass*," John was saying, quoting the words she'd heard in her head, just moments after quoting *other* words she'd heard in her head. "How are we supposed to know what that means?"

"I know what it means," Lisa told them. "Ask me."

SIX

The Idea

JOHN PACED. It dawned on him that he'd been in a weird honeymoon this last week ... but now the curtain was falling and he could suddenly see how odd and intolerable it had all been.

For the past week he'd felt safe, but that safety was just an illusion.

He'd been occupied enough to have some fun despite it all, but also deluding himself. If you were still making wagers while a hammer fell down on the world, you officially gambled too hard and too much.

John had been keeping his head down, dealing with the others in the hotel as if this was all just an intermission between a pair of sensible worlds. Had he really figured he could just wait here forever, and maybe the aliens would go away or stop mattering?

The others treated him like a leader, always asking him what to do. It felt nice enough that he'd let himself believe he really *was* one.

But John had never been a leader before. He'd always been last in line. Last to pay his rent, last to look his family in the eye and say he preferred them to the thrill of the hunt. Now he'd gotten used to thinking of himself as a whole new person, but he hadn't changed.

He was living a delusion on borrowed time.

No wonder he had no ideas. And no wonder nothing really seemed to matter. According to the original plan, it should have been adios for him by now.

He'd be dead, but Maria would still be alive.

Further proof that fortunes could always change.

It didn't matter how it'd happened. It didn't matter what John had believed without meaning to. It only mattered that the veneer was finally off, and he could see the world as it really was.

He wasn't John Abbott: High Roller and Leader of a Tribe.

He was *John Abbott: Degenerate Who Got Lucky Once, When it No Longer Mattered.*

And still, despite all that'd happened, his first instinct was to go downstairs, deputize Lisa as a dealer, and demand that Dennis return to Pit Boss duties so John could get back to the roll of a lifetime.

There was a goddamn alien ship in the lobby.

There was a goddamn *alien* — just the way the news described them — unconscious but apparently still alive beside his ship.

And somewhere out there, a creature the size of a Buick was prowling the streets, taking bodies and leaving heads to roll like forgotten bowling balls on the ground.

He'd been pacing all night. Over and over the same hundred yards or so, wearing the carpet in a circle. No sleep for John.

Those who thought they could rest had gone to bed long ago. Joanna had caved and asked Lawrence to sleep with her. Not like that, of course. John suspected marriage had imprisoned Lawrence in the Friend Zone forever.

They all needed comfort tonight.

He didn't know what to make of Lisa's story. Any other day of any other week, John would simply decide she was nuts and move on. But whereas even Jeremy could only read his notes about what Amerigo had recited, Lisa could still repeat the message word for word. Those who'd seen Amerigo's little ventriloquist act, with himself as the dummy, agreed that her version was more accurate. She'd gotten words right that nobody else could remember until they heard them.

She was right about the stones, too — one more reason he wasn't so willing to dismiss Lisa as totally loco. If she hadn't actually left the hotel, how did she know about the stones? He hadn't been aware of them until fifteen minutes ago, when sunlight finally kissed the horizon and he'd climbed to the roof deck — right where Maria jumped, he supposed — and looked out across the city.

It was mostly quiet. It could have been normal, even, if John looked away from the Strip to ignore the ruins and still-smoking ashes. From up high, the boulders impossible to miss. They didn't sprawl across the entire Vegas suburbs, but the rocks surrounded more than the Strip.

The giant monoliths made a circle, and while it didn't feel like a gate exactly, it did seem an awful lot like a fence. They were far enough away that Lisa had either sprinted blindly through the night in both directions or she'd been somehow teleported there, just like she said.

Teleportation? *Aliens?*

It was too much. Granted, the planet had known the aliens were coming for six days before they arrived, thanks to that Astral app so many people had on their phones, but still ... *gigantic what-the-fuck.*

Aliens were the domain of nutballs living in trailers and eating their meals off of hubcaps. The fact of their existence — right downstairs, no less — was suddenly too weird to fathom. Add in the puppetry that "little silver BB" had done with Amerigo, and an exponent got added to what was already so odd.

Amerigo had spent the remaining hours before retiring owning up to his role as alien communication vessel, going so far as to brag that he'd *always* been in touch with the supernatural. That was why he'd gone into magic. Amerigo even claimed that he'd glimpsed these specific aliens in the past, while doing ayahuasca, while his mind had split open to let the wonder inside it.

All horse shit, so far as John was concerned. Amerigo was the kid in high school who dressed all in black and talked about how the unreal was more real than the real so often that everyone made sure to sit spitball distance away. Now he was the adult who'd made a show-business career doing the same damn thing.

Amerigo had claimed to see more than he said aloud. He'd also described the stones, same as Lisa. Margaret, cynical of pretty much everything, had been dubious of the Magician's claims, saying he was simply repeating Lisa's words.

But John had been watching the unfolding and was quite sure Amerigo had been downloading an entirely different sack of shit to Dennis while Lisa was telling her story. Immediately afterward — without time for the Magician to catch up on Lisa's little narrative — he'd described the stones in exactly the same way.

What did it all mean?

John might be a colossal fuck-up, but at least he was rational. It was hard to make rational plans in an irrational situation. Eight hours ago, their decision was simple — and easy enough to implement, since Leader John only needed to say *okay*.

They'd stay put until they had a reason to leave.

Now they had all the "reason not to" they could ever want, and it was time for John's next and more advanced phase, but he was out of rope and hadn't a clue.

Option One — They could do nothing. Act as if the ship had never breached their perimeter, the alien had never arrived, Lisa had never gone missing, and Amerigo had never been turned into a human marionette by a massive muscular man and his pet ball bearing.

That option was the most tempting. It was also the most problematic and, John suspected, easily the stupidest. They'd survived thus far because Lucky's old-style construction made it a concrete fortress and because it was so far off the Strip that nobody felt it worthy of paying attention to.

Now both of those things were gone. Lucky's was no longer a fortress. It had a huge hole in its front and could no longer fly under the radar. People must have seen the crash. Both species would soon be checking it out.

Option Two — They could fortify and prepare for … *something*. The "something" was a shitty cherry atop an already craptastic sundae. Fortifying themselves against human intruders — those who'd burned the Strip, looters, or everyday assholes — sounded awful enough, but John was sure there was more to fortify against that they had yet to understand.

For instance, the alien message, delivered through Amerigo and heard somehow by Lisa, said the injured alien in the lobby would be retrieved. How, John had no idea. Was a mothership on its way? He'd seen footage of the vessel hovering over Vail, Colorado, and found it petrifying.

Would the aliens send another small craft — a shuttle? John didn't think so. There was already a shuttle in the lobby, and its door had closed on its own, barring entry or investigation. If it was a matter of shuttles, they *had* a shuttle.

That left the aliens themselves. In shuttles, on foot, or flying with capes like Kryptonian refugees, John had to assume they were coming. What would happen then, and how could they possibly prepare to defend against it?

Option Three — With Option One stupid and Option Two foolhardy, leaving the hotel was really the only choice that made any sense ... though surely that was foolhardy as well, if for no other reason than the message ordered them not to flee. At least inside Lucky's they had 1960s construction at their backs. Outside, they'd have nothing.

They had a few weapons — the one he'd been saving for suicide, Todd's firearm, Margaret's cannon, and theoretically Taylor and Olivia's shotguns, if the twins chose to come along. But he'd heard the shots outside and knew others had machine guns — even some echoing explosion in the outskirts that had to be an RPG and a ball of flame.

They were soft civilians, except maybe for Todd. Leaving home base was about the worst thing they could do. But they couldn't ignore the reality that home base had been poisoned as well. And of course they couldn't just run for the border, making for the desert and hoping open spaces might keep them safe. Those damn boulders kept the humans right where the aliens wanted them to be.

A gate has been established that you cannot pass.

Lisa said some internal voice had guided her through. It had supposedly let her pass the first time with impunity then promised the second time would not be so easy.

No clear winners. And yet Leader John would be expected to make the decision for them all. He'd be their scapegoat if the situation went snake eyes. There was no real way to win unless something changed.

"John."

Todd was at the bar, sipping morning poison in the dark.

Once the aliens arrived, Todd started drinking more than before, from usually to always. He hadn't been there on the last loop, John was sure of it. But now he was occupying a barstool, facing out instead of toward the walnut counter, with a posture of waiting.

"Morning," John said.

"That alien still out front?"

Well, no. It'd never been *out front,* though they'd also discussed dragging the behemoth into the street like sacks of garbage waiting for the sanitation truck. Maybe the aliens would retrieve it without bothering to enter. It made some sense, but they'd still have the ship inside and the aliens had promised "consequences" if they moved their injured fellow.

If it *was* injured. It might just be sleeping. Dennis had given it a cursory exam and declared it startlingly similar to a giant human body, then declared the alien alive and breathing, even if in long and shambling breaths. The thing had veins on its wrist just like a human and matching vessels on its enormous neck. Both showed a pulse, weak as it was.

Dennis had opinions but refused to give them without a prominent qualifier. "If they're like us, which they might not be at all …" He'd paused so they'd all be clear how tentative his prediction was. "Then I think it's gravely injured despite the lack of obvious injuries. Maybe blunt trauma, like it slammed around inside the ship, and maybe hit its head. It might be dying. If it's like us. Which it might not be."

And the message through Amerigo's lips — *this body is damaged* — seemed to agree.

Understanding his meaning, John said, "Yeah. I just passed it thirty seconds ago. The ship, too."

"I sort of had an idea." Todd seemed tentative, and it took a long second before he delivered the second part of his thought. "Remember when I told you about my cousin?"

"The Navy SEAL?" John asked.

"He's not really a Navy SEAL."

John waited for more. This seemed to be meaningful, but Todd would only stare at him as if expecting his new friend to fill in the blanks.

"Okay," John said.

"I didn't want to say anything earlier because I'm sworn not to."

"*Sworn*, huh?"

"I'm not fucking around!"

The sudden vehemence — so early, and John without any sleep — startled him.

He thought of Todd's personality as "socially bipolar," though surely that was bastardizing the concept. Todd could be calm and rational and sometimes the most solid among them, but that solidity came with a flip-side. He also had a grizzled-vet manner of snapping without any obvious reason, and a tendency to take offense when nobody saw it coming. His hands occasionally shook, though he didn't have palsy. He'd developed tics. John didn't like to turn his back on him.

"Take it easy. I just want to understand."

Todd nodded as if to himself, then continued in his normal voice.

"Look. My cousin. Francis. He does work for the military in a special capacity, but not in special ops. I told you all that because I needed a way to explain how I knew about the invasion before the public, and I figured, okay, sure, SEALs might be part of a first-response team for aliens. Maybe it was dumb. I've thought up plenty of better excuses since."

John was listening with his guard up. That snap — along with the other strange things he'd seen from Todd whether he'd admit them to Kristina or not — made him treat the guy like a grenade. He was powerful to have with them, but only if the man could be kept from exploding. He'd thought the SEAL story strange, but harmless. Just like Todd's assertion that he'd known about the ships two days before Astral had seen them. Some tidbits he'd tossed out made John believe it, though. Somehow, Todd really had known first. It'd been a useless datum until right now.

John sat and leaned in. Maybe Todd was off his rocker, but it's not like John was overflowing with superior options. He could listen to potentially new and valuable information.

"He actually works for a team that protects Area 51," Todd said.

It took everything inside John not to roll his eyes and moan.

Wasn't that an outdated response? Mentioning Roswell or Area 51 used to be instant conversation-stoppers. A toggle switch that flipped to show you were talking to a crazy person. But there really *were* aliens. By all accounts, the government *had* been keeping secrets.

"He works for Area 51," John repeated, trying to keep the skepticism from his voice.

"Not for it. For a team that patrols the base." He half-shrugged. "Maybe not 'patrols it.' More like, there are soldiers who patrol, and my cousin works for a government-owned security company that maintains the systems and teams surrounding it." Todd seemed to realize his explanation was unclear, so he made a visual. "It's like rings. Area 51 is here ..." He held up a finger. "Complex security — soldiers — are all around here." He drew a circle around the finger with his other hand. "And my cousin's bosses are out here—" He drew a wider circle. "— like secondary security, support, maintenance ... you get the idea."

John didn't really get the idea, but all that mattered was *Area 51*. "All right."

"I was just thinking. We've got an alien."

"Well ..."

"And what's at Area 51? Aliens, obviously."

John figured that was acceptable. He nodded, because why not.

"We've got an alien," Todd repeated.

"You said that."

"Don't you get it?" He grew more animated, half-standing from his stool. He was bald-headed but the look was strange on him, set off by a movie-star's face, bushy eyebrows, and tan Caucasian skin.

"We can't stay here, right? And we can't just walk out, either, or those rocks will blow off our heads."

"I don't know about that …"

"They said we can't 'go through the gate.' The rocks are the gate. Lisa said it fucked with her head when she went through, but it *let* her through and *we're* not supposed to go, *so* …" He raised those big eyebrows, apparently implying cranial explosions.

"I don't think I get the idea, Todd."

"We take it with us! We … we build a sledge or something, and we take it with us! They said they want us to leave it alone and they'll come and get it, but … *Look*, man!" He pointed, but they were in the bowels of Lucky's away from any visible windows. "Those ships are still flying all around, so why haven't any of them stopped to pick up their buddy?" He leaned in. "You know what I think, man?"

"What?"

"I think it's a test." He tapped the side of his head with a finger. "My cousin told me how he hears things because he's got security clearance to eat in the cafeteria out there with the other guys. He's not supposed to say shit, but we get to drinking and … You know how it goes. He's all buttoned up usually, but when he hangs he hangs, and he told me the aliens who came here before were always testing. You ever hear of Benjamin Bannister?"

Now John really had to fight to keep from guffawing. "The alien conspiracy" — he stopped himself from saying *nut* — "guy?"

"He's studied this stuff forever. And he says all these old signs, from all these old civilizations ... they all point to prior occupations, and all those times there have been testing. I'm not talking probing and shit. I'm talking about psychological tests. Moral tests. Tests to see if we're worthy."

"You don't say."

Todd nodded meaningfully. "And Paulie, he said that Bannister came to Area 51 as a consultant, claiming there have been abductions leading up to this. Sometimes they take people aboard their ships and probe them or clone them or whatever, sure, but sometimes they just snatch them and stick them in some sorta mindfuck. Like, they'll take a bunch of different kinds of people — types and beliefs and whatever that'd normally fight with each other — and put them in a human puzzle and see what happens. They just ... snatch them from their beds, throw them in these giant complexes with all sorts of different colors on the walls ..."

"Colors?"

"Yeah, like, you know how different colors are supposed to have different effects on the brain? Like blue stands for trust or whatever?"

"No."

Todd didn't seem to hear, or care. "Anyway. Point is, maybe this is a test!"

John's face fell. He'd been buoyed by a feeling that he was listening to nonsense without any point, but now he saw that Todd was actually, for-real, proposing a plan of action. It seemed to have its own internally-consistent Todd-logic. Hearing "maybe this is a test" put a period at the end of his sentence. It meant he had decided something, and John had a strong suspicion he was committed — not requesting consent so much as informing John of what was about to happen for all of them.

"I don't know, man. The message said not to move the body."

Todd slapped a hand on the counter. "Because it's a test."

"And it said not to leave the city."

"Because it's a test!"

John must have looked skeptical — and he very much was — because Todd calmed himself and situated his ass into a better position on the stool.

"What reason was there to give us that message at all? It just let us know all the things we can't do, and as much as I think about it, we've only got a few choices, and none of them are any good. We can't stay, we can't go … You know what I'm saying?"

John actually did. It had preoccupied him all night long.

"But at the same time, they're giving us this message saying, 'You can't leave.' Then Lisa gets teleported away somehow—"

"We don't know that she—"

"—and hears the *same* message, like word for word as far as we can tell, but she said it almost sounded like it was being recited, like a play, like it wasn't real."

"I didn't get the impression that—"

"But they put her *outside* the stones and told her to come back and let us know what she saw, heard, and felt. That sounds like a dilemma to me. You ever study logic?"

"No." And it was a shocker that, by implication, Todd had.

"It's a dilemma. They give us a set of orders, then show us a bunch of shit that casts doubt on the realness of those orders. 'You can't cross the stones.'

And then Lisa shows up saying she crossed the stones."

"But it also said that if she tried to cross them a second time …"

"They say, 'Don't move the body. We're coming for it.' But then a whole night passes and there's shuttles all around Vegas, and still nobody's come for the body."

"Maybe they have to send a bigger ship, and that takes time."

"They've been here before," Todd said, leaning in further. "I never believed it, but when Paulie got blasted, he told me some shit that made me start wondering if I was wrong and the nutbags were right. "They know who we are and how we think. Bannister said that there's a theory about how they maybe left stuff behind to track us, too. To monitor us between visits."

"That's just … insane."

He waited for Todd's explosion, but none came. Instead he was patiently watching John, making him feel like the unreasonable one — the one who'd been deluged with proof, yet still refused to believe.

"Fine. Maybe it is all crazy. Maybe Paulie's wrong and I'm wrong and Benjamin Bannister is wrong, and there's been nothing out there before now. Maybe it really isn't a test. Maybe they mean everything they said through Amerigo."

Todd stopped. John hated himself a little for his curiosity, knowing he'd paused with one big point still left unsaid.

"But?" John prompted.

"But what better choice do we have?"

SEVEN

The Bride

JOANNA FOUND herself caught between a rock and a hard place.

On one hand, she hated Todd's plan. But on the other hand, everything she proposed as an alternative sounded like cowardice more than sense. Her biggest suggestion for the group was to do nothing, hang back, and wait to see what happened … but that was inaction. Passive rather than active. Joanna thought that was okay. Sometimes passivity was the best choice. But when the comedy girl spat Joanna's own words back at her, she could actually hear how they had sounded.

Besides, nobody agreed with her. The refrain was now, "Fine, stay back. We'll leave without you."

But that wasn't Joanna's plan; her plan was for

nothing to change, and for *no one* to leave. She couldn't enact her very simple strategy if everyone else insisted on being proactive.

It was unfair. Why were her desires being ignored? She should have as much say about the group's next move as anyone, and yet the others apparently felt like they could decide for themselves … which, in a way, meant deciding for everyone.

Joanna could go along with the others as they tried Todd's dumb and suicidal idea, or she could leave the group and stay at Lucky's alone.

She'd apparently pushed Lawrence too far. Even he didn't want to stay with her.

She'd said *Go away* and he'd said *I'll stick around*, and she'd said *Go away* again and he'd repeated, *I'll stick around*. And then she'd said *Go away, God dammit. I really mean it. Stop playing hurt little puppy and saying you're sorry and instead just GET THE HELL OUT OF MY FACE.*

Now at the worst possible time, Lawrence seemed to have finally listened.

That would be bad — not just for her pride, but for her life, her future. Truth was, she did love Lawrence — just not in the same way he loved her. If her anger — which, increasingly, was turning inward toward herself — had driven him away, that would be tragic. Joanna would hate herself more than she deep-down already did.

She wondered what was wrong with her. She'd created the drama, then gotten ensnared by it. She'd flirted with Lawrence last night because it felt better than admitting all those alien ships were really here, then been furious when morning came and he'd wanted to play romance. She was a woman who'd intentionally cemented herself inside a building of concrete blocks ... then shouted that someone had trapped her. She always did this. It was her defense mechanism, she supposed, and she knew it, and she knew how bad it could make things.

Yet still she did it without fail. Happiness seemed to bother her deep down, because every time it came close, Joanna ground it into the dirt with her heel. Now she'd hurt Lawrence but couldn't drop her guard to admit it — to say that *she* was sorry for a change. Maybe she'd even pushed past the point of saving their friendship. Maybe she'd pissed *him* off. Maybe the shoe was finally on the other foot, and she was the transgressor while Lawrence was righteous.

Either way, Joanna had no allies. Imprisoned in a no-win situation.

For now she was solving the problem by pretending it'd never get so far as to *become* a problem. She sat in a corner with her legs and arms crossed, watching them plan, telling herself the aliens would arrive in the meantime.

Fate was against her, and noonday sun arrived not too hot or cold — just right for disobeying corpse-eating creatures who operated human beings like hand puppets and surrounded cities with psychic rocks that were far too heavy to lift.

Vegas looked like a postcard. If they turned away from the Strip, the view was still beautiful and not at all threatening. They couldn't see the rocks from Lucky's ground floor, so the streets away from the Strip could be anywhere. Nobody was out. Birds were chirping and little lizards kept scampering up outside walls. Margaret, who was usually as cynical as Joanna felt right now, even parked herself in a chair not ten feet from the big alien ship and laid back as if to sunbathe. The demolished entryway was awash in an apron of sunshine, and the warmth was almost enough to welcome them into the wider world rather than forbidding them from it.

"Joanna. You coming?"

Not Lawrence, but Jeremy. He was probably

seventy, maybe older, and had the look of a very handsome man who'd grown seasoned instead of decrepit with age. It wasn't that way for women. Joanna knew better than most. At age twenty-nine, she was nearly too old to model now, and deep down she suspected it was because she was far uglier than she believed. People around her just told her she was pretty because that's what you were supposed to say — but dammit if the Showgirl wasn't prettier, if fuller figured, and the Comedienne wasn't prettier, if too short. Even Margaret, the chain-smoker with skin like a gecko, had a look Joanna suspected tracked backwards through time to a young woman who'd been stunning before the tandem attack of gravity and time.

Soon Joanna would be thirty, then things would all be over — not just for modeling, but probably for her hopes of having a family. Nobody wanted an old model and no man wanted an old maid.

"Joanna?"

She had to stop this daydreaming. This nefarious self-doubt. It was making her seem even more vacant than they already all believed her to be. Jeremy was the most laid-back and optimistic of the group, and yet her dumb brain had made even him repeat himself.

"I guess I'll come." She heard and hated the whininess in her voice.

"Taylor and Olivia are coming with us, but the others in their group are staying," Jeremy told her. "They can protect you."

Protect me or rape me. She had no idea of their group dynamics.

"It's fine."

"Fine to go, or fine to stay?"

Dammit, Jeremy, let me have some *dignity.* "Go. Whatever. It's fine."

"All right, then. Go ahead. I'll take the rear."

"What makes you think I can't handle the rear?" Joanna asked, attempting to salvage her pride.

"Sure. You take the rear."

She pushed past Jeremy, past the big white alien on its improvised stretcher, and to the center of the pack. Lisa was closest to Lawrence, so she sidled up next to her.

He looked over at Joanna, surprised. She kept her eyes forward and pretended not to notice.

"You decided to come?" Lisa asked.

"Apparently."

"Good. I'm glad."

Joanna allowed her one-armed hug. Lisa had

befriended her early because demographics-wise, it made the most sense. Kristina was like bedding a cactus — nobody wanted to stay near that. The affection between them wasn't always mutual, but Lisa had thus far been handy when Lawrence wasn't a conversational option, and in moments of weakness, Joanna had even opened up.

Yesterday, after the marriage debacle, she even told Lisa that her primary feeling wasn't anger but fear. Joanna was scared she'd ruined the best and most genuine friendship she'd ever had. Worse, she *kept* screwing up that friendship and couldn't seem to stop.

Lisa suggested she just talk to Lawrence and tell him she had overreacted. They could go back to being friends if he would allow them to.

Joanna replied that Lisa should mind her own business and walked away, but Lisa, like past versions of Lawrence, always seemed willing to take her back. She even liked the Showgirl, though the feelings were complex. Lisa was prettier and younger than Joanna, and if the man here she was actually attracted to (Gambler John) was interested in anyone, it would be her.

But at the same time, Lisa seemed so innocent. Like despite her profession, someone who might need directions in the bedroom. Even their week-old friendship felt naive. Joanna's sex talk seemed to embarrass her, maybe because of her religion or maybe because she really was as innocent as she acted. Joanna kept expecting Lisa to ask to braid her hair. Or maybe they could get together and make friendship bracelets.

The first step in Todd's plan was to get the alien inside his armored car, which he'd taken out early and had to leave in a public garage when the streets to Lucky's filled with debris from the fire … and of course the gangs with their weaponry, hopefully all gone by now. They'd need to walk as much as half a mile with the alien rolling along on its stretcher — an hour of travel and logistics, perhaps, before setting out for good.

So Joanna dragged her feet, bringing their pair out of earshot. She shot a glance at Lawrence, then flinched away when he looked back.

"Lisa?"

She turned her head. All blonde curls, and yet as far as Joanna knew, she hadn't styled it since the panic started.

"Is this a good idea?"

"Todd says it's our only real choice. I think John agrees."

"That's not what I'm asking."

Joanna waited for her to understand. The only people with true, direct knowledge here were Lisa and the Magician, because those were the two through whom the aliens had spoken ... or teleported and shown dreams, or whatever. Everyone else was using thin logic to make flimsy guesses.

"It's as good as any, I think," Lisa said.

"That doesn't sound like a ringing endorsement."

Lisa shrugged.

Joanna decided to try again. "You said the voice in your head encouraged you to cross the line of stones, didn't you?"

"Sort of."

Dammit Lisa, stop waffling. "Did it or didn't it?"

"It said I *could* cross." Again Lisa described the feelings she'd had between the monoliths. Hearing it all again, Joanna did think it sounded almost like an assessment rather than an attack — a notion that squared with Todd's theory that they were being tested. "So yeah, I think we'll be okay. He — *it?* — said it'd be hard, not impossible like Amerigo ... whatever. It's the rest I'm not sure of."

"Which parts?"

"Pretty much everything else." Lisa's voice was

casual, as if merely conveying a curiosity. She wasn't looking at Joanna and couldn't see her expression — one that, if she had looked, would make her stop and act more concerned straight-away. "I think we'll be okay moving the alien. That feels optional to me — maybe part of the test or maybe not. But *where* Todd wants to move it?" She shook her head of radiant curls again. "I don't know. You know what people say they do in there."

"In Area 51?"

Lisa nodded. "Supposedly they do alien autopsies. I don't think they'd want anyone doing autopsies on one that's still alive." She looked skyward, as if to see whether the aliens had spotted them yet and, if they had, whether or not they cared. A shuttle buzzed overhead as if in answer, passing by like a tram on rails without even slowing. "But even if they don't cut it up, they pretty much have to imprison it. Conduct experiments or something."

"You think?"

Lisa shrugged. "That's what Todd thinks."

Joanna looked up at Todd, who stood out clearly with his gleaming shaved head. She didn't trust him but couldn't say why.

"Then shouldn't we take it somewhere else?"

Joanna asked. "Somewhere that won't piss them off?"

They'd heard two new rumors on the over-air radio a few hours ago that were front-and-center in Joanna's mind right now. One about shuttles firing death rays that vaporized their targets, and an extremely troubling, but fortunately dubious, one about the aliens dropping car-sized bombs that went off if and only if the populations around them behaved in certain ways — *which* ways, the announcer hadn't known or said. Both rumors were probably nothing, but still they made Joanna shiver.

"Where else, though?" Lisa answered. "I mean, unless we're taking it *to* somewhere, we're just dragging the poor thing around like luggage. If we aren't moving that alien to a place that cares about what we have, why take it at all?"

Joanna had been wondering that last part a lot. "Even if we get it there, what's to stop the military guys or whoever from just taking it and making us wait outside?"

"Nothing, I guess. I think Todd's just hoping he can find his cousin."

"Who's F-level there," Joanna countered. "It's not like he's a general."

"Yeah."

"That doesn't bother you? That they might not even let us inside?"

"I kind of *doubt* they'll let us inside. When the garbageman comes to take your trash, you don't invite him inside the house. Even if he begs. *Especially* if he begs."

"So why do you want to go?"

Lisa shrugged again. "What else are we going to do?"

It was maddening, how non-neurotic she was about all of this. Wouldn't *anyone* join Joanna in some good old-fashioned freaking out and worrying about things she couldn't change?

"But I mean, you sort of talked to them. You were sort of ... I don't know ... *in their world?*"

"Yeah. And I'm still alive, so there's a chance."

Lisa gave her a bright smile, but it was hardly the assurance Joanna had been hoping for.

EIGHT

The Pit Boss

DENNIS HAD EXACTLY one formative experience treating patients as a doctor.

Med school didn't count. Nor did his internship since because as an intern, he'd always been able to defer to another person's authority — the resident he was working under or, in the case of group rounds, the intern body as a whole.

With eight of them all guessing diagnoses, it felt safe to make mistakes. Same when he'd been making rounds with his resident. If he screwed up, his superior's double-check was always there to catch him. Despite those safeties, Dennis had never made mistakes. A few small ones, sure, but they were always caught — by himself — before leaving his lips. If he'd been on his own back then, he wouldn't have hurt anyone. *Nope.* That didn't happen until his first day on his own.

The very first goddamn day.

A patient presented with abdominal pain. He ruled out the usual culprits, including appendicitis. It was his call to treat, and he'd prescribed fluids and an anti-nausea drug that turned out to have a name very similar to a respiratory depressant.

The mistake was caught before anyone died, but it was a near miss. Dennis was chewed out, reprimanded, then sent back into the field even more exhausted and stressed out than when he'd made his mistake.

So he went home sick — a move that was frowned upon heavily, especially so very early in his career. He drew a warm bath and sat in it until the water went cold, realizing with slow and hideous certainty that he'd ruined his life. He'd sacrificed everything for medical school, including moving two-thousand miles away from family, friends, and even a boyfriend who probably would have become a fiancé. Once there, he'd sold his car, cashed out his savings, and still ended up $300,000 in debt by the time of his fateful bath.

I can't do this. I hate this.

And he realized that it wasn't a revelation at all.

He'd hated his path for years. For most of undergrad and all of med school, Dennis had loathed what he was doing. He'd never really wanted to be a doctor. Maybe a scientist — like a pharmacologist or a biochemist, making drugs to help patients instead of dealing with them directly … plus all the paperwork and insurance and legal hassles. His paycheck wasn't the stuff of legend. Dennis had anticipated his pending reality for years, and yet he'd kept right on paddling his canoe toward the waterfall.

He only had himself to blame.

A friend worked in Vegas. Dennis went to stay during a premature leave of absence that was really a breakdown, and supervisors back at the hospital had warned him that such a move might cost him future advancement.

Cool with Dennis. That was exactly what he was banking on. He ended up a blackjack dealer, then a pit boss shortly after that. Now here he was, thirty-five years old and doing a job he woke up for every day simply because it existed. He didn't even watch doctor shows on TV. It felt too much like staring failure in its unblinking eye.

So when they finally got the alien into Todd's well-concealed and hence unmolested armored car and asked Dennis to assess its condition, he reacted with the same gut-churning reticence with which he'd approached that first assessment.

He didn't want to do this, and if he hadn't let slip during that first evening of weakness that he'd briefly been a physician, he wouldn't have to.

But now, he was the group's medical expert. Dennis didn't want to work on people, so how the hell was he supposed to work on an alien?

"It's alive, though, right?" Todd asked, taking the driver's seat while John and Margaret unloaded bags full of supplies from the surprisingly well-stocked First Aid stores inside Lucky's. They were turning the car into an ad-hoc ambulance, or really more of a parody of one. "We can't trade it for asylum if it's dead."

Dennis had all sorts of doubts about that, and they all aimed in opposite directions. He had no faith that they could reach Area 51 in an armored car even though it was less than a hundred miles away.

He was less than sure that if they got there, that they could attract the attention of anyone inside without getting shot — if, in fact, there still *was* anyone inside, and if those inside-things were indeed interested in extraterrestrials.

He was dubious that Area 51 would want the alien — they must have others, right? — or that they'd let the alien-bearers inside as a thank-you just so they could take shelter.

He did, however, have a tiny bit of hope that the alien's being alive might make the difference. That's why he was here and it's why he was doing his best, despite the pressure and the loathing, to do his doctor thing and hopefully keep it breathing.

Because while the rumors about Area 51 seemed more likely than ever to be true, Dennis still didn't think they had a live one. They'd gotten lucky that the alien had crashed in a way that injured rather than killed it, and that their little bit of fortune had been delivered right to their doorstep.

Maybe that was a better way to look at things. They weren't cursed for this having happened, they were luckier than most. And yeah, maybe Todd's plan was a long-shot — but practically speaking, Dennis felt a whole lot better when trying to convince himself that it was a sure thing.

"It's alive, as far as I can tell," Dennis confirmed.

Margaret was stuffing medical supplies into the

money compartments all over the car. They'd lucked out there, too — not with the supplies. *Every* casino had basic medical supplies. But with their mode of conveyance. Todd's company served several local casinos, but he'd ended up at Lucky's. His car was still operational, and they'd reached it without incident.

An *armored* vehicle, *designed* to withstand a direct assault. If they had to take a road trip through what felt like hostile territory, this was the way to take it.

Margaret held out an IV bag. "Does it need fluids or anything?"

"How should I know?"

"If it were human," she said patiently, "would it need fluids?"

"It's not human."

"But if it were."

"But it's not."

"Shut up, will you?" Todd said from the front. "I'm trying to remember where I hid the keys."

Dennis wrinkled his brow. He'd seen Todd playing with keys back at the casino.

"Here we go." Todd apparently found what he needed then started the engine.

Margaret shrugged and put the IV bag in a compartment. Dennis had let them stock things as much as they wanted because it seemed to make the group feel secure, but he wasn't about to go sticking needles into an eight-foot alien that barely fit inside the vehicle. If it died for lack of fluids, they'd just have to prop it up for Area 51. Do a little *Weekend at Bernie's*.

The vehicle pulled out. The ride was impossibly tight, carrying a dozen humans and one alien. Dennis wanted to keep it flat because that's what you did in real ambulances, but limited space made propping the alien up a necessity. Todd was driving. Lisa was sitting with Joanna on her lap, and Kristina jammed between them. Everyone else was in the rear, packed like passengers on a refugee train.

The ride was surprisingly uneventful. The first five hundred feet made it seem like the whole errand might fall flat because the way was littered with burned-out wrecks and debris from what Taylor and Olivia claimed was a rocket strike.

Taylor said he'd seen it happen from a room on the Lucky's twelfth floor. Some ganged-up yahoos on the street with a big toy over one man's shoulder, shooting things because artillery was nothing if not fired. Jeremy said he remembered the sound one night and Amerigo claimed to have seen it in his dreams when he was communing with spirits.

That would have made Dennis instantly doubt all that Amerigo had said and done, if only Lisa hadn't experienced the same basic thing.

When they reached the stones, John from the rear and Todd from the front were the first ones out. With the back doors open and the confinement and heat of their situation alleviated, no one else seemed especially compelled to move.

John poked his head in, looking for Dennis. "Everything okay with the patient?"

"Why?" Dennis asked.

"If we think these rocks are ... you know ... psychic somehow ..."

John looked embarrassed just saying it.

Dennis let him off the hook quickly, even though he wanted to give all of his usual caveats ... *I don't know. How could anyone possibly know what's possible for aliens? I'm not a doctor and probably never wanted to be. Why are you making me do this? I'm on the edge of a panic attack, you know.* And so on and so on.

Instead, he said, "Yeah. It's doing fine."

John looked at Lisa. He was probably asking her how this worked or what her weird vision said about how this might or might not affect the alien — or

them, since they weren't supposed to be out here —
but she answered as if he'd requested directions.
"These are the rocks I saw."

One by one they moved toward the geological
line. Dennis held up a hand twenty feet from the
invisible perimeter and felt something like static.
That sense of potential that hits a beat before the
shock.

"There really is something here," Olivia said. "I
can feel it."

"What now?" Joanna asked, turning toward
Lisa. "Do we just … walk through?"

Misgivings were piling up inside him. Dennis
was suddenly sure this was a bad idea. They'd been
told not to leave the casino and they'd been told not
to move the alien's body. They'd been told, too, that
the city was being watched and the "gate" would
stop them if they tried to leave.

The aliens had promised consequences.

But John's gaze was fixed behind them. "Look."

The others did. Nobody gasped, though maybe
they should have.

John started out looking toward Lucky's, probably about to declare that they'd been wise to leave.
Nobody had ever shown up to take the alien as
promised. Now, he was looking above that at three

silver shuttle craft, slowly approaching, coming to rest a few dozen feet away, as if meaning to give the humans space.

"I think yes," Lisa said out of the blue.

Dennis turned toward her and away from the waiting shuttles. She'd spoken to Joanna but now turned to everyone.

"I think yes, we just walk through," she repeated.

"What makes you think they'll let us?" Taylor asked.

"Because I think I can hear them inside my head. They won't stop us. They're … observing us. They're …" She took a much longer pause this time. *"Curious."*

"I think so, too," said Amerigo. "She's right."

"This is what we're supposed to do?" Jeremy asked. "That's what you're getting from them?"

"Not exactly." The Magician shook his head. "It feels to me like they want to see what happens. But *as to* what actually happens?" He shrugged. Coming from someone with such a usually-dramatic presence, the everyday gesture was an anticlimax. "Who knows?"

"Well, fuck that," said Todd. "I got us here. I'm not going first."

"I will." Margaret finished her cigarette then flicked it onto the ground.

The Cynic

Because, really, I'm dead anyway.

Margaret considered the rocks, deciding if they were malicious, they'd be like in that movie *Scanners*. They wouldn't make her go insane or stop her heart. Nosiree, they'd pop her head like a pimple.

And that was just fine, because there were two Margaret Horns in this world. The first one had grown up poor, wrangled a scholarship to a snooty middle school with an impressive dance program, then moved out of her parents' dirt-floor shit hole without looking back or ever seeing it again.

For a while, that first Margaret — who, back then, lived in the same skin as the second one — had been happy and even excited about life. She'd done well in school and had a few friends. She'd discovered dance and dived in with gusto, devoting every non-studying, non-social moment to her new and eagerly embraced discipline.

At fourteen she moved from her preppy middle school to a similar scholarship at an even preppier high school. That's when things went bad.

Within a month, her social circle had decayed from the middle. Friends she'd had in middle school were at the bottom of the income range and thus shuffled back to public school once the higher tuition kicked in.

Margaret's scholarship endured, but by the time she realized what that meant, it was too late for crawling back to her parents and begging for the unrelenting poverty, harsh punishments, and a school that scraped the bottom of society's barrel but at least had her friends among its students.

Instead she stayed in the superior school, now with an even better dance program, and girls who could afford to both attend and abundantly shit on Margaret the Charity case.

They targeted her as if on a mission to prove they were different — that Margaret and her ilk did not belong. She was shamed to the back corner of every classroom, shamed into eating alone at lunchtime.

Dance fared even worse. The high school instructor was an old-school Russian with similarly antiquated opinions about eating disorders. Specifically, they were compulsory. Any dancer over eighty pounds was simply *not* a dancer.

Suddenly, after three years spent finding her

place, Margaret was all the wrong things. She was too fat and too stocky to dance — an opinion all the other dancers made sure she was aware of. She was too poor, certainly for any social activities, and much too ugly.

Looking back, that last made Margaret angry. She hadn't been ugly at all. She'd been beautiful — and not according to that everyone's-beautiful-in-their-own-way bullshit that was so popular these days. With the right leg up, she could have been a prized dancer. With encouragement, she might have gone into theater. She could even have modeled and made a mint — something she wanted to tell Joanna about, if only to steamroll her dreams, same as hers had been.

That year, the first Margaret died. The second had been living in her skin ever since.

The new Margaret was the opposite of the old one. Crude and soured before her time. Her words bit like vipers. She smoked like a chimney and had not one but *three* ex-husbands, all of whom were beer-slugging blue-collar Joes like her daddy, and all of whom had beaten her with wild abandon. Now sixty-eight years old, Margaret had settled into a dense core of jaded cynicism — the way a bright sun collapses into a neutron star when its life comes to an end.

So if someone had to die first, it was okay if it was this old and jaded Margaret. The Margaret who mattered was long gone. Maybe New/Old Margaret could meet her in heaven.

A hand settled on her shoulder. "You sure about this?"

It was Jeremy Barnett. The man was sweet, the two of them could have easily paired off. He was her opposite in many ways. Still optimistic despite his age and all he must have seen, silver-tongued with a silken voice where she was thick and hoarse. He was good-looking, too, and not just for a man his age. He might be fifty-five. Sixty on the outside. Whereas Margaret had felt at least near sixty-eight forever … and now that it was her actual age, she felt ninety and counting.

"Someone has to do it."

"I'll do it," Jeremy said. "I'm the oldest."

She shook him off. It was important to be clear and decisive. If she showed any hesitation, his gallantry would swoop in and insist she let him take the brunt of the blade. But Margaret wasn't playing. She *intended* to pass through the gauntlet first.

If she survived, great. She'd have proven her

value to the group and deserve their company. If she died? Also great, because life was a giant sack of monkey balls.

"Get off, Jeremy. I said I'm going."

Margaret stepped forward.

At first there was nothing.

Then it seemed like every hair on her head was standing on end, along with every vibrating follicle on all four of her limbs.

"You okay, Margaret?"

She didn't know who asked because they were very far away.

Very *very* far.

Margaret was suddenly adrift in a vast ocean, but the water below her boat — yes, she seemed to be on a boat — was bright pink. It wasn't blood unless it was the blood of something beautiful, like unicorns. Or Care Bears. Surely they bled pink.

Who are you? came something that was more feeling than voice.

Margaret.

Which Margaret?

The dead one. The old one.

Who are you, Margaret?

She turned around, seeing that her boat was one of

those yellow inflatable things with wooden seats they used for whitewater rafting. There was one person in the boat with her. Herself, smoking. Tracheotomy in her neck. If it'd been her other self's voice speaking moments ago, it hadn't sounded like a voice box.

But who cared? She was already gone.

What do you think, Margaret? asked her other self. She spoke without moving her lips — so no voice buzz at all. *Is this Heaven or is it Hell?*

There's no Heaven. No Hell.

Are you sure?

For less than a second, the tranquil pink ocean around her became scabrous red cliffs impaled with pitons the size of spears, their ends tipped with bone.

Fire blazed below, but only because Margaret expected it — or because society expected Hell to be hot and she was just playing along.

She felt no physical pain, but the mental agony, in that heartbeat of existence, was unbearably heavy.

She couldn't breathe. Couldn't move. Couldn't even think.

But then a horrible thought did occur to her. *I'll be stuck here forever.*

There was no way out. No escape. No way to die again.

Eternity was eternity. By definition, suffering was eternal.

Memories of her worst days came back to her magnified a millionfold.

She watched her infant sister born, grow a few years, then die.

She watched her mother's lung cancer as if from the inside, seeing its inevitability long before any living person had.

She saw days in the future — visions of hideous days to come.

Loneliness became a palpable thing, stripping the last of her hope.

In that blip she saw how her cynicism was a shell of protection.

Margaret believed in nothing because she was afraid to believe, so in that moment she *did* believe, and then disbelieved, and then was crushed beneath the weight of—

It was over.

Even the pacific pink expanse of water was gone. She was, instead, collapsed in an untidy pile on cracked pavement. She heard something, unable to understand what it was. Then she understood.

When she opened her eyes to see, still it took another thirty seconds to gather her bearings.

But then they came and Margaret realized she was back in Las Vegas, now on the other side of the stones.

"She made it!" Amerigo declared. *"It's safe!"*

But the Magician was wrong.

The Massacre

KRISTINA FELT the change not when Margaret raised her head and Amerigo Cross shouted, but well before that. She felt it when the stones seemed to release the Cynic from a grip that kept her upright, even as everything below her waist lost muscular tension, and left her dangling like something dead.

Margaret *fell* from between the rocks more than *passed through* them, and in that moment, Kristina felt something switch on. Not *off*, but *on*. Rather than trying the stones for the group, Margaret had primed them instead.

She looked at Lisa on impulse. It felt as if her head had been turned by something outside herself. She didn't like the Showgirl at all — for no good reason, but that was that — yet still Kristina found camaraderie in the other woman's gaze. Lisa, she somehow knew, was the only person she could have looked to when feeling what she had definitely just felt.

Lisa was the only one who'd understand, because she'd been there.

She was the only one who knew.

But it was too late. The black-haired twins pushed past Amerigo — who'd been preparing to sprint through before getting shoved aside — staggered, and almost fell.

Kristina opened her mouth to shout. She didn't like Taylor or Olivia either, but still she bellowed. Their motivations were suspect. As was their origin. They were a threat to the group Kristina had finally cobbled into a parody of trust, and she gave her faith to no one. Taylor and Olivia were outside. The others were inside. She'd never stopped looking at them askance — not for a second.

But she shouted anyway, feeling more than seeing the danger. Kristina had gotten too close, and when the force between the rocks expanded after spitting Margaret out, the feeling was like cranking an old speaker without any music, an ambient hum that permeated through a person's skull.

Maybe that was how Kristina knew they were heading straight to their deaths.

The twins hit the field in tandem, and the same force that had propped Margaret up took hold of them both, lifting their feet from the ground. They didn't go glassy-eyed like she had. The old woman's face had withered into fear, but the twins seemed scared from the start. Both were conscious, too, not in a trance like before. Their wide-open eyes glared into one another as they floated just a few feet apart.

The hum intensified, now audible for all of them. The nine people outside the open-backed armored car winced and leaned back — not scared so much as wary in an instinctual way, the way a predator instills fear in its prey.

Margaret's eyes were clearing. She looked in at them with abject horror, surely reliving whatever she'd just experienced.

"*Taylor* ....!" Olivia moaned.

Both of their eyes snapped closed. Their expressions clouded, faces contorting with discomfort. The hum continued to build, to build, to *build*.

Then it happened all at once. Olivia seemed to

concentrate and Taylor seemed to concentrate, and then they simply detonated like bombs.

Not just their heads — every single cell from top to bottom. It wasn't even blood that splashed the rocks in a big red wave. Its color and consistency were off. It was probably plasma and a slurry of cellular detritus. Saline and ruptured cell membranes and all those microscopic organelles Kristina had learned about in boarding school. The endoplasmic reticulum — both smooth and rough, naturally. Ribosomes. Centrioles. Golgi apparatus.

Taylor and Olivia hadn't just been liquified. It was more comprehensive than that.

Someone shrieked. It might have been Joanna, but it also might have been Todd.

For a few moments, chaos reigned.

It was impossible to tell who was talking, or where, or why, or what they were even doing, or what city this was or what time of day.

Kristina distinctly remembered her last comedy show, but it was as if she was *there* — not because the rocks were mind-fucking her, but for a much more serious reason.

She was building herself a mental cocoon because she could no longer comprehend her true surroundings.

She pulled herself back, with effort.

It felt like leaving her crowd hanging.

It felt like refusing to answer someone's question inside a dream, then wondering in a sleep-addled state if she was being rude.

But the effort paid off, and soon Kristina was blinking in the morning light, trying to recall the dual realities warring for her attention.

The rocks. The rocks are real, and the show is not.

But weren't those audience members waiting for Kristina to take the stage? Wasn't that none other than Heather Hawthorne, her idol, watching from the rear? She couldn't stop now. Reality was no fun.

But this was. Couldn't she stay just a little while longer?

Come back, she told her self. Come back, girl.

She did, and immediately had to lean, then fall to sitting. She wasn't alone. Only John and Dennis were still upright. Joanna's mouth wouldn't close. Lisa must have been too close to the explosion — she was red with gore.

The blood wasn't viscous enough was the problem. Plasma was made of charged cells and had strong surface tension. This was more like mineral spirits, thinned into barely a skein.

After long minutes, they began to stand.

"No way," John said. "No way we're going through there now."

Jeremy blinked until he found his sense. "What about Margaret?"

"What *about* her?" Amerigo asked.

"She's stuck over there?"

Lawrence, frazzled and far out of character, said, *"Who fucking cares?"* His arm wrapped around Joanna, and it looked as if she might not even realize. It was unclear who was comforting whom — who was keeping whom from falling.

"We have to go back. And Margaret ..." John looked between the rocks at her, in apology. "Margaret, maybe you can get help?"

"You sent me through, and this is what I get?" she yelled back.

"You volunteered!" Joanna said.

"Hey, fuck y—!"

A scream tore through the chaos.

Kristina saw a blur. She turned to realize it was Todd, who her last glance had registered as rising by himself against one wall, both hands shaking, his expression a mask of fury.

He'd been psyching himself up — for a berserker run, apparently.

He sprinted toward the line of rocks.

Several people shouted for him to stop, but he'd put momentum behind himself, making it impossible to stop in time.

He gave a mighty bellow as the hair on his head began to rise with static repulsion, and when he hit the field's center, a force inside swept him upward, same as it had with the twins.

His feet left the ground, but only barely. His eyes slammed shut as Margaret's had. His mouth twisted. His hands gripped nothing. His legs stuttered as if receiving a shock.

"It's going to happen again! Get back!"

But before anyone could move at Jeremy's shout, Todd's palsy ended.

And same as Margaret, he was hurled through to the other side. He collapsed in a pile not far from her, then took his time rising in a daze.

Margaret glanced over at him like he was either a hero or a fool. Then she looked at the others.

"He's okay," said Lawrence. "Why is he okay?"

Todd was mumbling, stumbling as he tried to rise. He found his feet while still bent at the middle, then overbalanced and crushed a stack of cardboard boxes against an exterior wall.

Kristina looked at Lisa. Every time she'd done so in the past there'd been a clever insult in the offing. Yet this was dead serious and nobody expected jokes … so Lisa seemed confused.

Jeremy said, "Maybe the twins were too slow. There wasn't time for Todd because he went so fast."

Joanna shook her head. "Margaret went slow."

Shouts overlapped.

Kristina kept watching Lisa. The Showgirl was inching closer, holding her hands out to feel that static tingle. Kristina thought she might go next.

"Forget it," said John. "We're not doing that."

"You mean *you're* not doing it?" Lawrence said. "Sounded for a second like you were deciding for everyone."

"We'll go back. Figure out another way."

"Maybe …" Amerigo didn't look cool or frightened at all. Just scared. "Maybe we can go over them."

"Oh, sure," said Kristina. "With a slingshot."

Margaret and Todd were talking. His eyes were huge, more off-balance than ever.

"Lisa," said John, making her jump. She pulled her hand back and looked accused. "What do you think?"

"I … I don't know."

"You've been through it."

"I don't know."

"It was only a second for all of them." It wasn't clear if Jeremy was talking to one of them or to himself. "You only have to last a second."

Lisa fixed on him and said darkly, "It's longer than you think."

"I say we run for it." Amerigo nodded emphatically. "We either make it or not."

"I'M NOT GOING THROUGH THERE!" Joanna shrieked — at him, but sort of at everyone.

Lawrence tried to comfort her. She punched and pushed him away. *"GET OFF OF ME! I'M NOT GOING!"*

"Shhh. Joanna. What choice do we have?"

Kristina barked laughter at her new husband's dumb bravado.

"What's the holdup?" Todd called from across the gulf. "It's fine!"

"It's not fine," said John.

"It's fine!"

"Someone has to drive my truck over, at least!"

John looked back at the armored car with its open rear doors. Something made him look at Lisa. "Hey. Do you think, if we took the alien and … ?"

A forest of rustling erupted behind them — clicks and the crumpling of huge sheets of otherworldly paper, the sound of a million locusts thrown into a bag and shaken. John stopped mid-sentence, glancing back before Kristina looked back herself, then refused to acknowledge her eyes.

She'd be paralyzed if they were right.

But if she kept ignoring the truth, she'd be dead.

A line of enormous black shapes were leaping over wreckage and short buildings behind them. A hundred at least. They didn't all fit down the streets, so those choked out of alleyways climbed whatever was in their path instead.

They looked like a cross between roaches and squids, all legs and something like long tentacles waving wildly behind them. They moved like insects, too — swift motions of too many limbs, darting movement, stop-start locomotion.

In daylight, the aliens were more obviously nightmares. They had mouths that opened almost flat with rings of pointed teeth inside. When they screamed — to counterpoint the rustling of their approach — it seemed to rattle the bones at the back of Kristina's jaw.

Todd and Margaret were standing now, seeing the insectile things and waving their fellows frantically forth. The scene to their rear was a portrait of hell. Something from a deranged artist's most twisted dreams.

Kristina counted one breath, two. Even that double barrel of beats seemed to last an eternity. She heard Lisa's voice from moments ago, now with a double meaning.

It's longer than you think.

The words made her remember the rocks. The reason they'd come here, now their best motive to run away. Or so it had been. Until now.

What choice do we have? Lawrence had asked Joanna.

In reality, they'd had all the choice in the world.

Nobody sees a gun on the floor with a note on it that says, *Shoot yourself.* and thinks, *Well, okay, sure — what choice do I have?*

What *choice?*

ANY choice!

They could walk away.

They could make a new home inside Vegas instead of crossing the Human Vitamix and ending up like Taylor and Olivia.

What choice *did they have?*

It was a moronic question — or had been, just seconds ago.

Now, the choice really was between the fat and

the fire. Ironically, the death machine in front of them looked like the least of evils.

The others started to scramble.

In the heartbeats it took Kristina to decide where to go and what to do, she saw Joanna and Lawrence rise and run in unison, bound at one hand, each with firm yet opposite intentions.

Joanna ran toward the rocks. Lawrence ran toward the monsters.

They reached their mutual limit and jolted hard at their held hands, almost falling.

Lawrence was waving her down, down … not *into* the creatures' attack but somehow *beneath* it.

Only … where was there to go?

Dennis had lost his goddamned mind. He screamed by, causing her to forget all about Lawrence, Joanna, and their conjoined dilemma. His war cry became a grimace of tension as he struck, then tumbled through the rock field.

Seconds later her head whipped in the opposite direction.

A scream that turned out to be from Jeremy, who'd chosen the opposite path and lost. One of the black things already had him, and was shaking his corpse like a dog with its catch.

Go, Kristina. GO NOW!

She knew in some animal part of her brain that the best option was forward. Lawrence might think he could get somehow around the line of those black things, but to her mind, there were far too many.

No hope in that direction. At least the rocks gave her a chance. So far, two had made it and two were dead. Her odds were no worse than flipping a coin.

But she also knew she was dangerously close to losing her nerve. And while dying by teeth or dying by explosion were both unappealing options, the worst of all would be to not even try — to die by indecision, seeing the blade fall and watching it happen.

So she made her feet move before cowardice set in. She pumped her legs, which weren't used to the effort. Kristina was slim, but accidentally so. She hated exercise but had lucked out in the genetic lottery.

Adrenaline filled the gap between will and way, keeping her buoyed through the seven or eight lunging steps it took for her to reach the alien gate.

Seven … eight …

Time slowed. Her last stride felt like she was dragging a foot through cold honey. She began to arc more upward than out, her hair rising from her shoulders, her hands tingling. She was able to look back one final time to see the black creatures now less than half a football field away, but even they already appeared to be winding down like a failure of Earth's grandfather clock.

… *nine* …

She was sitting at the head of a long table — one so long it was like something from a cartoon, a graphic novel. Its surface was also slightly trapezoid-shaped, wider at Kristina's end than the other.

At that opposite head was her mother, dressed in a blood-red dress with a collar so high, it was like something Dracula's wife might wear. The fabric looked stiff as plastic, shiny like the toe of a new boot. Mother's makeup was more severe than in life. Eyeshadow that made her eyes look like ochre pits, lipstick as bright as her dress, shadows drawn on her cheeks that made a seven on the right cheek and a backwards seven on the left from where Kristina was sitting. Cheekbones sharp enough to slit a man's throat.

The table's surface was the deep gray of Father's best suit. Two candles burned on either side of a large candelabra. On the table was a banquet like their private chef had never cooked.

There was something trussed and brown like a turkey, but it wasn't a bird. A ham, but it didn't look like the leg of a pig. Something with the consistency of mashed potatoes, except it was light gray and studded with tiny wet peach things that ran red on one side. The butter wasn't butter. It looked like huge scraped away flakes of mold, rolled up and compressed like a remainder soap made from the last of a thousand bars.

Her own hands were flat on the table before her — one on either side of Mother's best china, which in turn was flanked by her very best flatware. A crystal water goblet sat at the one o'clock position, to the right of a small fork polished so bright, it hurt to glance at. Her napkin, still atop her plate and folded into a swan, was filthy. It looked like it'd been used to staunch a wound, then left for days in the sun.

Her hands were far too small ... until her memory changed and her perception changed and she began to see them as just right. Of course they'd be small. She wasn't an adult yet. She was eight, maybe nine,

... *eight* ... *nine* ...

and now the woman at other end of the table was no longer her mother, but Heather Hawthorne.

She was already speaking. Words Young Kristina hadn't heard. She picked up her speech mid-sentence.

"… and I mean impossibly hard. You'll want to slit your wrists. You'll want to blow your brains out. Even when a set goes well — even when you kill out there — they'll talk about you. They'll whisper. You can never just be you. You always have to be someone you once were, that you hated. And—"

She stopped.

As in frozen.

As in, someone had hit *Pause* on the world.

Kristina found herself talking like a little girl. "Could you please pass the rolls?"

Heather was right beside her. "Girl like you? They'll eat you alive. They eat *me* alive. Every day I'm more dead than the day before. There's no more life. Just degrees of dying. You'll marry well or you'll die in the gutter. Mommy and Daddy told you that, didn't they? Like a bedtime story. Like the monsters in your closet, which by the way are *very* real. They said 'a girl needs her man.' Because what are you without someone acting as your backbone?"

And Kristina answered, "I'm my own person. I don't need anyone."

"Then stop pretending. Stop pulling your

punches. Hate is the only reason your star is rising. Hate is the only reason the casinos started booking you. Hate is the only reason you're blowing up online. Maybe there was a day when well-balanced comedians could make it, but the days of comfortable humor are long over. You want to make it in today's world, little girl? Then never stop wanting to kill yourself. Mommy did you a favor. Every day you want to cry is money in your pocket."

Now Meyer Dempsey was beside Heather. Husband and wife, holding hands.

"You need a team," Meyer told Kristina. "Because out here, you can't hang yourself without someone to hold the rope."

Kristina looked down. Her plate was full of blood, wicking slowly up into the soiled napkin so that the swan seemed to be gradually going under. Her bread knife had become a box cutter, her forks now tiny pistols.

"You don't have to die," said Heather. "You just have to make it hurt."

Then she rose, turned, and leapt atop her husband, their faces mashing into a grotesque kiss. They pushed onto the table as if they were one body with eight limbs, sending the plates of strange meat and sides to the polished-wood floor.

Kristina pushed back in disgust as the candles fell too, one rolling from its holder to ignite a set of pitch-black curtains against a faceless window.

As she pushed, Kristina saw that she now had adult hands, adult forearms. Slit from wrist to elbow, open on the dorsals side in long, lipless mouths.

The box cutter was askew, no longer neatly beside her plate. It was covered in blood, pressed with Kristina's own filthy fingerprints.

Her head swelled with pressure.

She had to end it. She had to end it. She had to—

"Holy shit, are you okay?"

—*end it.*

She blinked up at a blue sky. Desert sky. John Abbott above her, not Mother, not Heather Hawthorne, not Meyer Dempsey. She had a heart-beat of confusion, one of calm, then a third beat of abject terror.

And it all came back at once with the force of a head-on collision.

She didn't sit up so much as scamper back.

Hands and feet in a crab-walk, backward like a ghoul from a horror film. She stopped when she struck boxes. The same ones, she realized, that

Todd had canted into. Only, they were soaked in red, same as the pavement around her.

"It's over," said John. "It's over, okay?"

The air was entirely silent. No rustling of rushing creatures, no screams of fear, not even the stepping of feet. Kristina could hear wind and birds, no more. It might be any day anywhere, ever.

She sat up and saw.

It was over, all right.

TEN

The Armored Car Driver

TODD LOOKED at his still shaking hands.

For a while it felt like nerves, but even after taking long breaths when the air finally cleared, he still couldn't get them to quit. It seemed unfair. A man should be in control of his own body. But when the others began to stop panic-fleeing and stir toward the resumption of a rational world, Todd moved his hands beneath his ass and sat on them. And still it felt like they were trying to get away.

Kristina, the comedy girl, had finally stopped mumbling. She was talking to people, it seemed, but not to anyone here. To *Mommy* and *Heather* and *Meyer*.

John had gone over and was helping her up, but Margaret was watching her almost as if she understood. Todd looked away — the Unhappy Couple, Joanna and Lawrence, were in matching fetal positions, practically sucking their thumbs — and when he looked back, Margaret was whispering something to Kristina … or asking her a question. Whispering close, in her ear. Something about what she'd seen, done, experienced.

Todd kept his focus outward. He didn't want to turn inward — not one tiny bit. Lisa said the time between the rocks lasted longer than it looked, but for the driver, it'd been days. Weeks, maybe. Even years.

Time in that place had been strange. An accessory to reality rather than dictating it. He'd had the distinct impression, before finally emerging, that some intelligence inside had been sampling time. Not obeying its relentless flow, but engaging minutes and seconds only when desired.

He'd seen his partner die, over and over again.

He'd seen himself shot, die, come back to life, then live for months in a hospital — little of which had actually happened — over and over again.

He'd been the bullet. He'd ridden the bullet. He'd been a small speck inside Hayward, his partner, during the robbery, that had witnessed its gory intrusion.

From inside his partner's body, he'd watched the bullet slide through human meat, puncture Hayward's beating heart, and come to rest inside his spine. Poor bastard never had a chance.

"What ... What happened?"

Nobody answered Kristina fast enough, so she asked more questions. Joanna and Lawrence were alive but seemingly catatonic, with zero signs of stirring.

"Where did those things go?" She seemed to remember harder with every passing second. Her face had grown agitated. *"Where are they?"*

"Shhh. They're gone."

But John's answer didn't please her. Todd could see her eyes, recognizing the expression clinging to her visage because it was the one he always saw in the mirror. She didn't want to be patronized or condescended-to, even in the depths of her frightful disorientation.

Kristina slapped his hand away before it could come to rest on her shoulder.

"They stopped at the rocks then crawled into buildings." Margaret's sandpaper voice was matter-of-fact — not because this was no big deal, but seemingly because there was something on her mind. She was still assessing Kristina, her look more curious than suspicious.

"When?" Kristina asked.

"A minute or two ago. You took longer than the others."

Kristina's eyes were still wild. "What? Why?"

"What did you see in there?" Margaret asked without answering.

Joanna was stirring. She looked at the red-splashed boxes and pulled back. "What the hell is this?"

"Amerigo," Todd answered.

Dennis was on a crate ten feet away. He had a hand to his forehead as if staunching a headache. "They stopped at the rocks like Margaret said," he told anyone who cared to listen. "Hard to believe they couldn't just come through. Makes me think they didn't want to get us so much as force us to make a choice."

"They said we couldn't go through at all," John said.

"It's a test." Todd swallowed. "Like I told you."

"What test?" Lisa asked.

Kristina's head whipped toward Lisa, and her relief was unmistakable.

Maybe after what just happened, relief at anyone living made perfect sense.

"What do you mean, 'Amerigo'?" Joanna asked while Lawrence finally began to sit up.

"Amerigo didn't make it," Dennis answered.

"Anyone else?" Kristina asked.

"No."

"Well …" said Margaret.

"And Jeremy," Dennis amended. "But those *things* got Jeremy. He never made it to the rocks."

There was a long moment of silence.

Todd's gaze made a circuit. Now they were down to eight — himself, Dennis, Margaret, Joanna and Lawrence, Kristina, Lisa, and John.

A third of them gone, just to leave the city. Not a good sign.

"Now what?" Kristina asked.

"Same plan," said John. "I guess we're committed now."

"But the alien …" Kristina stopped when her sweeping eyes found the armored truck, still idling with its front end kissing a bodega wall. She looked at Lisa, who'd started to fidget. "I figured if we had to cross those damn things, then their buddy should have to do it, too."

THE ARMORED CAR was true to its name — *armored*. It'd taken a good front-end hit when Lisa drove it through, but was still just fine, with barely a dent on the thing. The stones had slowed it a little, but Lisa had really slammed the pedal and the strike had been enough to easily crumple a normal sedan.

Todd, driving now, wondered if maybe Lisa had been onto something. To him, the truck had barely seemed to slow. Maybe that was the way they should have gone all along — and, if you believed some of those still living, maybe that was what the aliens wanted. If it was a test, like Paulie would say, then maybe this particular trial was about disobedience and guts. Maybe they weren't even supposed to pause. Maybe they were supposed to keep their hands and legs inside the vehicle just like on a roller coaster, and blow through full-speed all at once.

Well. Too late now. They were north of Vegas and, once clear of the outskirts, seemed not to have a care in the world. They were heading into nowhere, so there was no traffic. A few cars by the side of the road, but nothing impassable. Todd might be his own father, at the helm of a family vacation in their old RV. When the eight people behind him got loud, he could just turn his head and shout at them to be quiet just like Todd's old man had always done. He could threaten to *turn this car around*.

The truck was low on gas, and that might be a problem. Apparently things like stopping were only issues when there were others around. The first station they found once leaving incorporated land was a four-pump outfit with a tiny store and a pair of abominably filthy bathrooms. The power was off and the place was abandoned, but the surrounding land was clear enough to ensure no invaders were coming.

Radio was still on-air. Todd had been listening while the others were in the back squabbling and learned a few things of interest. First, predictably, marauders were a genuine threat. There were a few reported cases of alien-on-human violence, but almost all issues right now were being caused by humans clashing with humans as the planet lost its collective mind.

The few alien reports so far sounded no more credible than UFO conspiracists before Astral Day and, said many, might be baseless rumors. Officially, no contact with the ships had been made — which made their own situation both curious and notable. To Todd, it meant his idea to take their patient to Area 51 was a good one. Without aliens even officially on the ground yet, the fact that they had one — an *alive* one, at that — might just impress the military after all.

He'd heard reports of stones, though. Nobody so far had seen the rock lines being built, but people were comparing them to something called the Carnac Stones, in France. Apparently strange geometry — and impressive, ancient-impossible feats of earthmoving — were alien hallmarks. He'd heard Benjamin Bannister's name brought up again, and each time the guy sounded a little less crazy to Todd.

Stone lines were appearing in many places across the world, according to the voice on Todd's radio. In the United States, they'd for some reason proliferated most around Moab, Utah, and Vail, Colorado. Vail was of particular interest in the alien conspiracy community, though it wasn't so much a *conspiracy* anymore, but Todd didn't understand why — just that lots of new-age folks were packing up tents and heading there for some sort of apocalyptic Woodstock. Apparently they thought Vail was an energy vortex of some kind. Better than Sonoma, it seemed. Todd heard "energy vortex" and stopped listening. Bunch of hippies felt Vail was their new Mecca because some crystals said so? Um, okay.

He'd take the credible coverups at Area 51 over that bullshit any day.

Curiously, despite numerous reports of "strange lines of enormous stones," nobody was reporting anything like what they'd just been through. He'd managed to catch video on a tiny antenna TV at a quickie roadside stop and even seen footage of people walking around the stones, right through the lines. No hovering bodies, no catatonic stares, no exploding corpses. The reporter said other stone lines were causing "general confusion" for those who got too close, and one report said a line near Boulder was "impassable" — literally, it seemed, as if the empty space between stones was a wall. It made Todd wonder. Was their line special? Could they maybe drop the rocks like Swiss Army barriers, and use them anyway they wanted?

Todd slowed, then pulled into the gas station. They all crawled out, stretching once they saw sun. It was, at least, more comfortable inside now. It felt disrespectful to say but was no doubt true.

"It's so nice out," said Joanna, looking up at wide blue sky. "Hard to believe we're in danger."

"Maybe we're not," said John. "Maybe there's nothing out this far."

A shuttle whizzed by overhead with a sound, as

if calling his bluff. Headed east, perhaps slightly north. Toward Vail.

When it was gone, the air was quiet again. Lawrence returned from wherever he had walked off to. "Power's off."

Todd said, "We figured that. I'll see if I can find a hose."

Lawrence had been blocked by the truck's side. He raised a hand, and Todd saw he'd found a hose already. A garden hose, maybe hooked out back for water. That would work fine once they cut it. Siphoning gas from other vehicles was bad enough without having to suck down thirty feet of fumes first.

"Excellent. I'll drive over next to that pickup."

He reached for the door, but Margaret stopped him.

"I got it," she said. "You take five."

"You know how to drive something this big?"

And Margaret said, *"Please."*

He walked across a dirt-skimmed parking lot to the convenience mart, casting glances into the broad, desertlike land around just in case others had decided to sneak up. It wasn't even ten. If they didn't run into trouble, they'd be at Area 51 by lunchtime.

"Found the key," said Dennis, picking a palm-sized rock from the ground.

John reached past him then pulled the handle. The door opened with the tinkle of a tiny bell. "Unlocked. Guess the clerk didn't care much about security at the end."

The engine Margaret had started turned off outside.

Todd looked back to watch her get out, open the gas, then take one end of the hose while Lawrence kept the other. Lawrence put his end into the tank and reached for the opposite end, but Margaret waved him away and put her mouth to the hose. Cool lady. Todd was starting to like her.

He looked back to see Hayward James, his old partner, standing at the end of the snack aisle.

His stomach plunged. Hayward's body began to elongate and change color. His clothes were melting into his skin, turning from mocha to snow.

He was growing taller, too. Now seven feet at least, on his way to eight. His curly hair was moving backward into his skin — a thousand hair follicles sucking back a thousand errant spaghetti noodles.

But through it all he had the gunshots he'd seen when Todd had first laid eyes on him. One in the center of his chest, broad in scope but not too deep.

He'd been wearing his vest and this armor round had punched right through. The second wound was in his temple, bleeding down on his bleach-white and hairless skin.

"You a Cool Ranch guy or classic Nacho?"

Todd spun to find the Showgirl behind him. She was holding up two snack-size bags of Doritos, one blue and the other red.

Heart hammering, he looked back, but Hayward was gone.

"What?" he asked her.

"You okay?"

He looked again. Just an illusion. Just a waking dream. He'd had them all the time before therapy, but therapy hadn't lasted long. Someone found out he was nuts — seeing things, unable to sleep, jumping at shadows — they'd never let him carry a gun. The armored car job was the only one he'd been able to get with his credentials — high school dropout, no special skills, good reflexes, and a sharp eye. If he wasn't meant for security work, what *was* he meant for? He needed that job. How else would he pay Laura's tuition?

None of that mattered now. It was the end of the fucking world.

"I'm fine."

"You sure?"

"I'm sure. *You* sure?"

Lisa looked disarmed by the ask-back. She nodded. Then she pitched her voice lower. "You used to be a cop?"

"Yeah."

"John says you know someone where we're going. Like a guard."

He nodded.

"Military?"

He nodded again. It was kind of true. Paulie's employer was military-owned, if not official. "Why?"

"I'm just a little freaked out, is all."

Todd looked around the little store. It was almost too small for privacy, but Joanna had already grabbed food and water and left. Kristina wasn't far behind. John was still inside, but he'd stuck his head out to call to Lawrence and Margaret, to ask if they wanted anything particular from the store.

Todd looked back at Lisa. He knew what this was. She was scared, and he didn't blame her. He was scared himself. Maybe more than she was, though he couldn't admit that. Because right now, she was speaking to him not as a person, but as a security blanket. If he'd been a cop — and if he now carried a gun, and knew a man who, she'd assume, carried a *bigger* gun — that made him an authority in a world where authority was either defunct or had gone missing.

What Lisa wanted right now more than anything was for Officer Todd to tell her that everything was going to be all right. Even if she knew it was a lie — and in Todd's mind, odds were 50-50 — she wanted to hear it.

"We'll be okay." He held up a map he'd grabbed from a stand near the door, which he'd already opened and refolded all wrong. "GPS isn't working, but looks like we're maybe fifty-sixty miles from where we need to be. It's all open land. Desert."

"But don't you think people will want to go to Area 51? I mean, everyone knows …"

Todd was shaking his head. "One time when I visited my cousin, the guy who works there, we drove out and laid on the hood of his cars and drank until we couldn't see straight anymore. Like, enough that we had to sleep it off in the car before driving home." He shook the map. "Yeah, everyone knows about Area 51. So *of course* the real stuff doesn't happen there. They use the same airstrips as before, near the salt flat, but where Paulie took me was about ten miles west. Separate roads and every-thing. Even if all the kooks *have* flocked to Area 51, it's not the right place. Hasn't been since the 80s." He shook the map again for emphasis, then tried on a reassuring smile that felt like wax lips. "The roads will be clear all the way to the gate. And—"

Outside, Dennis was running and shouting.

ELEVEN

The Patient

"*Gauze! Anything!*"

John watched Dennis run — first toward him as he stood rooted halfway between the store and the truck, then past him.

He watched as Dennis burst into the store, slamming the door hard against a rebounding wall. The works shivered but no glass broke. It seemed a miracle.

"What happened?" John asked.

Kristina — her posture that of a smoker on break — answered. "Something with the thing inside."

"What thing inside?" He was looking at the store, through the glass, seeing Todd and Lisa's surprised faces as Dennis rushed in and started raiding the shelves. His compass was all screwy, assuming "inside" meant "inside the convenience store" because he'd already been keeping an eye on Todd and thought this might be the unfortunate dawn of whatever he'd been watching *for*.

But despite Todd's strange behavior — not to mention jumping at shadows, as he'd also done *inside* moments ago — it was clear Kristina meant something else. Something in the other direction.

His head spun 180 degrees, then back to Kristina.

"You mean inside the truck? *The alien?*"

Kristina shrugged.

John rushed past, around to the rear doors. He found Joanna with her hands splayed on the alien's chest. It was horizontal now, occupying most of the floor space. Joanna looked disgusted and her hands were covered in what was probably blood, but she was still dutifully doing what someone — Dennis, almost for sure — had told her to. Lawrence was across the body from her, also kneeling, seeming to be looking for something to do. Margaret was outside with her feet on the blacktop, watching.

"What's going on?"

"It just started bleeding," Margaret said from beside him.

"What cut it? How is it bleeding?"

"How the hell should I know?"

John climbed into the armored car.

He surveyed the scene with a feeling of panic — a look reflected on Joanna and Lawrence's faces, if not on Margaret's. They'd discussed this exact scenario before the stop, and the discussion had unequally divided the group.

The majority — John, Dennis, Joanna, Lawrence, and Lisa — felt strongly that if the alien died, their quest perished with it. Area 51 felt like a long-shot no matter how they hurled the dice, and though John didn't want to bring this up, the fact that the plan depended on Todd was a serious strike against it.

With the alien alive, though, their odds struck John as still fair. Capturing anything alive was harder than capturing it dead, so it *may be* they had something even the military hadn't seen.

But dead? Hell. Everyone knew Area 51 had *dead* aliens. Todd hadn't heard the conversation. Margaret and Kristina felt it didn't matter whether the thing lived or died, but their opinions were easy to dismiss because Margaret and Kristina were basically the same person thirty-five years apart. A pair of cynics who didn't seem to believe in anything.

"Is it dying?"

"How should I know?" Joanna answered.

Lawrence put fingers to the thing's neck. "It has a pulse."

Margaret scowled. "So? For all we know, having a pulse is a bad sign for them."

"I've got an idea how to cure it," said Kristina. "Hit it with a rock."

"Shut up, Kristina," said Lawrence.

"Oh, and you know?"

"I know that bashing things with rocks doesn't help them, no matter what they are."

"I see. But how can you be sure without trying?"

John looked back, ready to add his protest to Lawrence's, but something in Kristina's eyes stopped him. Before the stone line, she'd been professionally jaded. The kind that made her the performer she was. Now, though, her edge was sharper. Broken and angry. What had happened to Kristina in the barrier?

Dennis rushed around the open door with a hand full of supplies, Lisa and Todd on his heels. They joined Kristina and Margaret, watching outside, while Dennis climbed in.

"Band-Aids?" said Lawrence.

"And gauze." Dennis's tone was no-bullshit, don't-fuck-with-me-right-now. "Lift it."

Lawrence did as he was told, raising the monstrous lower back so Dennis could slip a wad of medical gauze underneath it. He made one circuit, squirted most of a tube of Neosporin into the gaping wound's general area, then packed it with a handful of cotton balls. A few more wraps concealed the blood. The creature was left with stained skin, a body wrap, and a cushioned tumor where its wound had been.

"Wow," said Kristina. "Well done. Neosporin *and* Band-Aids."

"I'm doing my best."

"We have legit supplies in all these drawers, you know."

Dennis looked furious — the kind of rage that comes only hand-in-hand with feeling stupid. He'd forgotten, and he was angry. Not just at Kristina, but at himself. They'd spoken, briefly — enough that John knew why the man had quit medicine. Of course a mistake was enraging him. The only one to take it out on was himself.

"It's fine," John said, looking from one to another. "Antibiotic, packing the wound … Not sure Dennis could do much better."

He looked at Dennis, but the doctor on duty wouldn't take his compliment.

Into the silence, Kristina shot off her mouth. "It's going to die. And good for it."

"It's not going to die," said Joanna.

"I say we roll it out now. Get back our leg room."

"Then what do we show Area 51?" Todd demanded.

"Come on." Kristina rolled her eyes. "You believe that horse shit?"

"My cousin works there!"

"So what? You cousin sounds like a mall cop!"

Dennis was silent, staring at the alien. "I ... I can stitch it."

"No, Dennis. You did good," John said.

A flash of anger, then back to focus. "I should stitch it. Thing's got blood, right? And it's got skin and a pulse and it even looks like us. Maybe we're related way back like the nut-jobs say. Who knows? When a wound is big, you sew it up. Makes as much sense for them as it does for us."

Margaret laughed. "That doesn't make sense at all."

"You got a better idea, or you just want to crap on everyone else's?" Lisa, shocking them all.

Nodding to himself, Dennis said, "I wasn't thinking. It wasn't cut! How could it just start bleeding?" He nodded more. "Yeah. I should stitch it. Maybe I can irrigate a little, see what's opened up. But at least I can stitch it."

He reached into one of their stockpiled drawers and pulled out a pair of bent-end surgical scissors. He slipped one end under the gauze and cut it away.

The cotton wadding was soaked enough to drip. It'd stopped being individual balls and was now just a mess. He lifted it up, then threw it out the back.

The wad just missed Kristina, who flinched then gave a dirty look.

"Hand me a bottle, Lawrence."

"Which one?"

"The one with the nozzle on the top. The squirty one."

Lawrence handed it over. Dennis directed a stream of water at the alien's wound to clear the blood and investigate the deeper wound beneath … but there wasn't anything there.

"What the hell?"

"Wh …" John was looking, too. "Did you lose it? How can you lose a wound?"

"Maybe if you retrace your steps, you'll find it,"

said Kristina. "It's always in the last place you look."

Dennis grabbed more cotton balls, sprayed them with the water, then wiped the alien's chest clean. It was completely unmarred, rising and falling.

"What … *What the fuck?*"

Then John saw something from the corner of his eye — a tiny flash of silver. He focused, stared, then felt a chill.

Soon they were all seeing it — a small sphere made of the same metal as the alien shuttles. It looked exactly like the ball that had possessed Amerigo and made him read the alien warning.

Then, in less than a blink, it accelerated through the open doors, flew into the sky, and was gone.

"Okay," said Joanna. "What the hell was that thing?"

Todd was looking skyward, seeing it go.

"They're watching us," he said.

The Experiment

They hadn't yet left. Dennis wanted to be sure the alien was stable before moving it, but that was dumb for a half-dozen reasons in Margaret's opinion. First of all, it'd healed itself, which wasn't miraculous. It was terrifying. If the aliens had come to conquer the planet — and why else, Margaret wondered, would they come? — then Earth was about to war with something that could seal up its wounds lickety-split.

But even if it needed time to heal beyond zipping itself up, the implication that Dennis or anyone else would know what "stable" meant for an extraterrestrial was ludicrous. What, was he going to monitor its vital signs? It might not even *have* vital signs. What Dennis took as heartbeat and respiration might be their version of tumors. Or it might already be dead. Had Dennis thought of that?

Kristina was sitting behind a rock, smoking a cigarette she'd liberated from the convenience store.

"Who's Heather?" Margaret asked.

Kristina looked up. To Margaret, the woman looked like a girl. She was small and waifish, with a hard edge, like a teenager in her *me* phase. Maybe she hadn't had time to mature emotionally, or maybe this was just the way things were now. The world changed too fast — and yes, Margaret was quite aware that was an old-lady thought if ever there was one.

She didn't care. It was true.

And here was another one: Progress — all that change — wasn't necessarily for the better.

"What?"

"Heather," Margaret said, moving around to face her. She leaned, but did not sit. "You were saying something about Heather after you came through the stones."

"Nobody."

"*Nobody,*" Margaret repeated, disbelieving.

"My sister."

"Really."

"I see. You're psychic. Are my answers not matching the ones on your cheat sheet?"

Unfazed, Margaret continued. "You also said 'Meyer.'"

"I'm a huge fan of the Oscar Meyer Wienermobile. Check out my weenie whistle." And she raised a middle finger.

Instead of being offended, Margaret laughed and stayed where she was.

"Can I help you with something?"

"Why are you all by yourself?" Margaret asked.

"Don't you like time alone?"

"Sure."

"Then fuck off."

Margaret waited. Kristina finally looked up at her and said, *"What?"*

"I know a little about you."

"Good for you."

"I saw your show. The last night at Lucky's."

"Yeah? Save the stub. It might be my last."

"It's funny. And I know you're a fan of one of my favorites."

"Stalin?"

"Heather Hawthorne."

Kristina looked away, taking a puff.

"You remind me of her. You're just as pissed off."

"I'm not pissed off."

"Really."

"I'm just realistic."

"I see. What are you realistic about?"

"Who are you? My shrink?"

Margaret sat opposite her. Kristina looked away again, annoyed.

"I've been talking to the others."

"Good for you."

"When I went between those rocks, whatever's in there showed me my worst memories. My worst thoughts about myself. It's like it held up a mirror."

"Mirrors were before your time, though, right?"

Margaret ignored her. "I used to be really interested in the occult. You know, there are some people who say the vampire myth is really just about abnormal psychology. It's a creature that feeds on the energy of others. A creature that hides and attacks by stealth. A creature that can't look into a mirror — not because it's invisible, but because it can't stand to face its own reflection."

"Fascinating."

"That's how it felt for me, the more I think about it," Margaret said. "That thing in the stones wasn't telling me anything I didn't already know or believe. I don't think it *created* anything. I think it just knew me better than I knew myself. So more and more, I think that what it did wasn't meant to torture us on its own terms. I think it lifted a mirror to our faces and asked, 'Can you stand what you are?'"

Kristina puffed. "What's your point?"

"When I told some of the others what I told you …"

"Which others? All of them?"

"Lisa," she said. "John. Joanna. Lawrence."

"Did Joanna's show her herself without makeup? Without her hair done?"

Margaret ignored that one, too. "When I talked

to them and told them my theory, they all picked up on it right away. I think it reveals who you are, but also what you think. What you believe, even if you don't believe it. John was cagey — and I don't blame him; I was cagey with him, too — but I think he's got a pretty bad gambling problem. I think before this whole alien thing happened, he was pretty close to the end of his rope. Lisa saw her parents, who disapprove of her career choice, but I actually think it was showing her what she thinks her parents are like rather than what they're *actually* like. Same with Dennis. He supposedly dropped out of medical school because he couldn't take the pressure, but what he saw in the stones was all about incompetence. He's not incompetent. That thing with the alien and forgetting to stitch it up? I think he knew. Deep down, he knew something wasn't right, so he 'did it wrong' so he'd immediately have to back up and 'do it right.' If he hadn't, we'd never have checked on its wound. We wouldn't know it'd healed, and we never would have seen that little spy thing flying around."

Margaret was far from sure that the ball bearing had been spying on them, but it felt right. Kristina didn't ask.

"I'm saying I think Dennis is a good doctor. The

mistake was thanks to his competence."

"That's great," Kristina said. "Tell it to the malpractice board."

"So I've got this theory that all the stones are doing is reflecting us back on ourselves. They don't show us truth. They show us what we *believe* to be true. How we feel about ourselves and our world."

"What about the people who died? Taylor, Olivia, Amerigo …"

"I don't know Taylor and Olivia. Who knows what was in their heads. But I talked to Amerigo quite a bit back at Lucky's. He saw me as a mother-figure, I think, so when he wanted to bitch and I was feeling low, I let him. It worked for us both."

"Beautiful. Did you fuck him? A 'Harold and Maude' sort of situation?"

"Amerigo had a lot of problems. Mother issues."

"Join the club," Kristina said, drawing another puff. Her last words were less combative, as if finally starting to listen.

"That's exactly it. You've got parent issues. Lisa has parent issues. Yet both of you were just fine and Amerigo wasn't."

"And I suppose you've got a theory."

"I do."

"Based on anything, or just hot air?"

"Based on what Lisa told me about when they first took her away and poked around in her mind. Things that sounded a lot like what Amerigo told me after the alien spoke through him."

"Okay. What's your theory?"

"I think they're interested in us. But not just 'interested,' like they want to know us. It's more like you'd be 'interested' in what drives a psychopath to do the things he does. Or, better, *What if there was a whole race of psychopaths?* You wouldn't study a group like that just to see what happens. Assuming you wanted to interfere at all, the first thing you'd probably do would be to try and save them from themselves. It's like putting an asylum inmate in a straight jacket, so they can't do any harm — to themselves or others."

"Great theory," Kristina said.

"But you're the one I can't figure out. Those of us who survived the stones all have some way to deal with their issues, even if it's unhealthy. I'm cynical. I hate everyone and everything, and don't believe in much anymore, though I used to believe in a lot. I'm dysfunctional, but I 'work.' I'm not going to do anything stupid."

"Whereas Amerigo …"

"He was in his upper twenties, but he never felt older to me than about thirteen or fourteen. I did a little volunteer work back in the day with troubled youth, and that's exactly how Amerigo seemed to me. If he were in high school, I'd worry about him shooting up the place. If he was dating someone, I'd worry that he'd become obsessive and controlling. The kind of story that ends up on the six o'clock news."

"This is great stuff. Really."

"You feel about the same to me," Margaret said.

Kristina laughed, then she looked Margaret hard in the eyes. "Okay. What about Todd?"

"Todd's single-minded about our trip to Area 51. Lisa thinks they'll let him have it, just to see what happens."

"Oh, *Lisa* thinks it? Must be true, then."

"Todd doesn't need to believe in anything else. Everyone here is just sort of hoping this will turn out, but he's convinced. It gives him purpose."

"That's why the aliens let him through instead of blowing him up like Amerigo? Because he's driven and has purpose in life? Maybe the aliens should write a self-help book."

"John's all about leading this group. Lisa — forgive me, but she's just too innocent to cause any problems. Lawrence and Joanna have each other, messed up as that whole thing is. I think Dennis is bent on redemption. Once he got through the stones and they held up his mirror, I actually think it gave him some confidence. He's much more attuned to his 'patient' now than before. It's like he's stepping back into his role — or at least the role this group needs from him."

"What about you, if you're so broken?"

"Keeping everyone at arm's length keeps me sane, but Amerigo kept everyone at arm's length, too. Honestly? I think my 'thing' might be this."

"Really. Your 'thing' is trying to explain what the aliens want from us?"

Margaret nodded without irony. It was true. She, too, felt more purpose now than before. More and more, she was starting to suspect that the line of stones — for them, anyway — was closer to tough love than punishment. Sure, it could turn to punishment in a blink, if for other reason than that scientists seldom felt sorry for their lab rats. If this really was some sort of big experiment for them, that didn't mean it'd last forever.

That's why the way they approached Area 51 seemed to matter so much. That would mark the end of this particular mission. There might be no reason to keep the subjects around once they had finished with their work.

Margaret held out a hand. Reluctantly, Kristina tossed her the pack of cigarettes and a book of matches.

"I get it," Margaret said. "You don't like me because I'm just another mirror."

"Got me all figured out, huh?"

"But try to meet me in the middle. Because as far as I can tell, you're the only one here without something to drive you. You *don't* have purpose."

"Now you really sound like my father."

"So that's why I'm asking what the rocks showed you. You came out of it clearly upset, saying two names I know — *Heather* and *Meyer*. I was able to get a signal on John's phone about an hour ago, and I looked to see if there was news about Meyer Dempsey since the invasion. Or his ex-wife, but Heather's lesser known than he is, even now. There was nothing on her—"

Kristina shrugged. "Sucks, right? InvasionGossip.com has really been off lately."

"—but I did find something on Meyer. Might be the last article ever written about him. Or published, anyway. It wasn't just about him, but it was about New York notables. Whoever wrote the article thinks he went west. He had a plane in Jersey, but then the flights were grounded. One of those 'sources close to so-and-so' says he's been obsessed with the idea of safe haven out—"

"Aren't we all?"

"*Before* the Astral announcement."

Kristina stopped. That'd gotten her.

"So?"

"I'm a big Heather Hawthorne fan. She's about the only one who can get me off the slots when I'm in Vegas. I think it's because I'm just as foul-mouthed and jaded. I know she was supposed to have a big showcase in LA because that's where I was headed after stopping at Lucky's. But I also know that everyone says Meyer and Heather are still together. That he's cheating on his wife with his ex."

"This is all so great. Thank you, Margaret."

"I'll just say it. I can't figure out how you made it through those stones. Everyone who did was either okay with themselves or has something else they're gunning for. Everyone except for you. You seem to hate yourself, and I still don't think you believe in anything — not anyone here, not our trip to Area 51. Am I wrong?"

"Are we still in America?" Kristina asked.

"What?"

"You heard me."

"Then yeah, but—"

"Then it's my constitutional right to hate myself, hate you, and generally be an asshole. I don't need your psychoanalysis. I didn't ask for it and don't want it."

But when she turned away for her next puff, Margaret swore she saw the Comedian wipe away a minuscule tear.

She looked back a second later. "Are you still here?"

"You misunderstand," Margaret said.

"I wonder why. Is it because you don't make a single goddamn bit of sense?"

"I'm not telling you anything. I'm asking what you saw in the stones, and if I'm right or wrong."

"Forget it."

"It's important, Kristina. I think it might be very important."

"Why?"

"Because if you didn't pass the stones' criteria and they let you through anyway, there must be another reason. That in there?" Margaret pointed toward the armored car, meaning the alien. "It's too weird. It's wounded, then it's not? It crashes right in front of us and actually falls right out of its ship ... but then the ship seals up and it all just sits there? We're warned not to touch it and they'll send others to get it and that we shouldn't leave the city — that we *can't* leave the city — and then what? Nobody comes or bothers us at all. Then when we finally decide to leave Vegas, what happens?"

"Monsters come to punish us."

"Except they didn't cross their own line. They just drove us right through it. I'm sure I'm right about this."

"Oh, you are?"

"Yes. Because I'm the Cynic. My role is to be suspicious of everything. John's the Gambler, so of course he'd green-light this crazy plan. Todd's a loose cannon — chaos to keep us on our toes. This group isn't random. It's like we were put together for a reason."

Kristina laughed harder than ever. When she calmed down, she took another puff and her face again grew serious, jaded, downright hateful. "You're crazy."

"Lisa agrees, and she's seen inside their mind. Lisa says something *helped* her to cross. Something ... unusual. She and I talked about all of this, and it sounds as right to her as it does to me."

"Then Lisa's crazy, too."

Silence lingered between them longer than the cigarette smoke.

"I'll say this much, and this much only," Kristina told her. "What the stones showed me? It wasn't encouraging. It's not a 'mirror' I'm looking back on now to find new purpose. So what's that tell you?"

"That maybe you're the control."

"'The control'?"

"If it really is an experiment, there has to be one person who's not actually part of it. There has to be one person who shows what happens if the experiment affects nothing at all. In this case, it means you get to be an asshole and stay an asshole. You're presented with the test but are also immune to it."

"What's that got to do with Heather and Meyer?"

"I think there's another possibility," Margaret said. "If you're here and you shouldn't be, then you *could* be the control. That fits."

"Or?"

"Or ..." Margaret cleared her raspy throat. "You could be the spy."

TWELVE

The Spy

TODD DIDN'T LIKE IT.

Something changed when he went between those stones.

There was always noise in the background now. It was as if someone three blocks away had their radio on, and some special geometry of the neighborhood had conspired to bounce its sound directly to him — routed through enough reflections that he could neither pinpoint the source nor truly hear the specifics.

After an hour, he'd begun to make out some of what was being said on that distant radio ... then felt disappointed because it wasn't a distant radio at all. Just the people in the back of his truck yammering on.

He kept his eyes on the road after that, listening but not really, paying most of his attention to the for-real radio and any news it might have to offer.

But during their long stop, Todd realized he could still hear those voices.

He could still hear Joanna and Lisa and Dennis and John even when he was in the convenience store and they were not. Before the alien had started hemorrhaging or whatever, Todd had been face-to-face with Lisa, staring into her big blue eyes. That was the first time he noticed it for real. That while her lips were moving and saying one thing, he could also hear her saying something else. Low, like a whisper.

After Dennis insisted they all wait to leave — *And why not?* he'd said. *The weather's great and there's not an alien or any people around.* — Todd did something he'd never done before in his life. He walked away from the group, sat cross-legged on a rock, and closed his eyes to meditate.

He didn't know how. Were you supposed to chant? Put your hands palms-up on your knees, put middle finger to thumb, and say *Om*?

While deciding, though, the question answered itself. He was suddenly hearing the voices better. Seeing people — people who were not himself —

better. The phantom radio was at full volume now, and the quieter Todd made himself, the better he could hear.

Most of all, he heard Margaret talking to Kristina. Saying, *You're the spy.*

And Todd didn't like the idea of a spy. He was an up-front, cards-on-the-table sort of fellow.

He opened his eyes to see Hayward standing right in front of him, clear as he'd been inside the market. His head wound was seeping. Todd thought he could see a heartbeat through the wet circle of blood in his chest.

"A rat, huh?" Hayward said. "We don't like a rat."

It was true. They didn't. Cops had to trust the people around them with their lives, and there was no way to verify every little thing. You had to let go of your skepticism in the line of duty, essentially handing a gun to your fellows and hoping they wouldn't point it at your head. Without trust, there was no brotherhood. No sisterhood.

Trust was everything, and a rat was the opposite of that trust.

"Margaret is guessing," Todd told him.

"You sure about that? Seems to me if you've got

the internal radio, they all got the internal radio. You walk through those doodads and *BAM!*" Hayward slapped one hand sidelong across the other. "Now you're magic."

Todd suspected he was spiraling into something like insanity. He knew Hayward was dead, had been for *years*, and he also knew that talking to one's dead partner — or, if this was the other way, talking to oneself — wasn't something normal people did. But nobody had to know, so screw it.

"You know what you think?" Hayward asked him.

"*What* do I think?" Todd asked.

"You think Margaret's got access to more than just hunches. You think someone's ratting right into her."

"That's ridiculous."

"As ridiculous as you listening in on their conversation right now? As ridiculous as you knowing that Joanna just asked Lawrence if he wanted to try sneaking into the gas station bathroom for a quickie?"

Oh. Right. Todd did remember hearing that one. He'd thought it was hilarious, because he personally had dropped an enormous deuce into the men's room toilet and the thing wouldn't flush. How romantic. And how scandalous, seeing as she was supposed to hate him!

"So you agree," Hayward said. "You agree that you know it."

Todd shrugged.

"What'cha gonna do about it, then?"

"Get rid of the rat? Leave her behind?"

"No. No." Hayward seemed very disappointed. "It's like you don't listen at all. Think through it again."

Todd did. It took more focus than he wanted to exert, especially if he still had an hour or two to drive and the station was apparently all out of Red Bull. His brain was tired. It'd been through too much. A feeling of narrow escape had left him shaken.

He dreamed about getting ripped into a thousand pieces like Amerigo and the others, but this — this right here — had somehow saved him. As soon as he'd started thinking again about a trip to Area 51 and their potential salvation, that sense of imminent death had disappeared. Purpose gave him life. Same for dedication. And he was damned if some spy was going to steal that away from him.

So Todd tuned his dial precisely. Listened to

Margaret and Kristina for a while longer, then, when she was alone again, listened with all his might to the Comedian. He knew what he was doing, even though it was crazy.

He was reaching his fist shoulder-deep inside her mind. The rocks had connected them all to each other ... and to some degree, connected them all to issues beyond their little group. Some were slower to recognize the truth than others, was all.

A moment later he *was* Kristina. Just at the surface, but plenty able to see.

She was thinking about a drug. Brewed from a plant, drunken, then purged.

He saw a door swing open inside her. Saw an unknowing part of her —suggesting she didn't even *know* she was a spy — reach out through that door and into the wider thoughtsphere.

Did Kristina know that particular drug had opened a door for the aliens to see right back? Did she know she'd opened a portal? That all that hippie shit about collective minds maybe wasn't such shit at all?

Meyer Dempsey. Heather Hawthorne.

She was thinking both names in a loop, driving Todd's attention to madness. She was trying to make sense of them after all Margaret had said, but doing it with half of her brain in bondage.

Heather was someone Kristina had always admired. Another performer of the same stripe, or so Todd thought. She had waved Margaret's questions away, but was right now wondering if any of them might be worth answering.

I never met Heather, but Heather's more mother to me than my mother. That's why I dreamed of her. That's why the rocks showed her to me.

Todd nodded as if it was his thought, but he was only an observer.

And Meyer? Kristina now thought.

The pause was longer. Apparently Kristina didn't know what to think of Meyer's intrusion into her thoughts — because, Todd now saw, the rocks had shown her this "Meyer" person as well.

The thoughts grew confused. He was new to this mental fuckery and had trouble keeping up. Despite Todd's best shamanic focus, he couldn't hold his hand inside his mind. Kristina kept flitting through ideas like an old-fashioned Rolodex.

Heather, as she was on television.

Heather, as seen from the front row, when Kristina had spent far too much on tickets as a nobody.

Meyer, in a luxury van.

Then back to Heather. In a red leather outfit with an impossible collar at an impossible table. Kristina's nightmare as she crossed the border.

Heather, her style and routines analyzed in full by Kristina's studious hand.

Heather instead of her mom. A better mommy than Mother.

Heather as prominent. As central. Far *too* central in Kristina's mind, really, to make much sense.

Meyer with Heather and a shaman, also taking the drug.

The aliens.

Meyer.

The aliens.

Vail.

The aliens.

Heather.

Meyer.

Then a place neither of them — not Todd nor Kristina — had ever seen. A city with a crystal pyramid. Vail with a veil. Heaven. Those hippies, making their journey to a place of vortexes and vibrations.

Kristina connected by the same tether as the

others. Meyer was a window because he'd taken the drug. Kristina was a window because she'd done the same. She was Heather Hawthorne's biggest fan. That's how she knew — even though nobody could know in any rational, normal-five-senses sort of way, Kristina included — that Heather had somehow seen the Vegas Strip as it started to burn.

They had a link. Somehow.

Meyer. It's all about Meyer.

But not just Meyer. There was — there would be — eight more.

Suddenly Todd's internal vision became less a thing he was part of and more a thing he was observing. He felt himself pushed out, from first-person perspective to third, then apart from it entirely.

He saw Kristina's eyes in the darkness, staring right at him.

Todd's real eyes snapped open as he startled and rolled off the rock. He hit one arm, then his shoulder, then his head. When he came up, disoriented, he blinked, unsure of what he'd seen.

He looked at the real Kristina. She had risen from where she'd been sitting and was now looking all around as if for an intruder.

"For you," said Hayward.

"Does she know?" Todd asked his dead partner, staying low so she wouldn't see him. "Does she know I saw all of that?"

"Does it matter?" Hayward asked.

Todd gazed across the desert. Getting left out here would mean death for sure.

You couldn't expose the rat. You couldn't let the vermin know you knew what it was or what it might be doing. Instead, you had to play the game and stand ready to catch the rodent as it sprung. That might be harder with this particular rat.

Kristina was their leak. She took a drug that created a window, and now they had open windows everywhere. Anyone who'd ever sipped the medicine had seen the eye of God ... and as it turned out, He had been looking right back.

It was true of Kristina, and it was true of the two other people she was so obsessed with — the woman more than the man. But it wasn't Heather that mattered. It was *what Kristina's connection to Heather meant* that mattered.

It meant the aliens had eyes everywhere. They knew so much ... and, Todd somehow seemed to know, they had been watching for years.

Centuries.

Untold numbers of millennia.

Area 51 was either salvation or a trap.

It was their plan, known by the aliens ... or designed by them.

"What does it mean?" Todd asked his partner.

But Hayward was gone.

THIRTEEN

The Ambush

THE ROAD from the gas station on was bumpy. The sun out here was a strange thing. Lawrence felt quite warm standing directly underneath it when there wasn't any wind, but even the slightest breeze made him wish for a sweater. He and Joanna were from the midwest, where weather was absolute. Here, it was capricious. Maybe the day star warmed you up, maybe it didn't. And the hotel had shown him how cool it got at night.

It dawned on Lawrence that he might die. He wasn't pessimistic enough to think the odds were in death's favor or anything, but it did feel possible now in a way that it hadn't before. Prior to the announcement that alien ships were on their way, death for Lawrence was an academic construct. An idea as blandly interesting as another person's suffering. Even after Astral Day, but before the ships arrived, it remained so. Some burned-out relay inside his mind refused to connect the idea of dying to himself. This was still essentially true after they saw the first ships followed by their first in-the-flesh aliens, because they were all too hopped-up on adrenaline and problems to solve that there wasn't time for thinking.

But there was time now, and Lawrence found himself looking at Joanna, whose refrain since yesterday morning had been that *she* couldn't die still married to him. They might not have much time. They might, in fact, have very *little* time. After seeing that little flying BB again, everyone agreed that the thing was either autonomous or being controlled by someone, and that in either of those cases, it pretty much had to be reporting to someone on the alien side.

And if that was true, what else was true?

More than half the crew was now preoccupied with a singular idea — *If the aliens knew what they were doing and remained interested in what they were doing, didn't that suggest they* approved of, *or at least were okay with, what they were doing?*

And might it follow, then, that this wasn't their

own plan they were following, but that it was, in fact, part of a larger strategy concocted by the aliens?

Discussion in the truck raged in one direction, then the other. Ironically, because they had nowhere else to go, they argued over the alien body. What sense did that make? If it ever got out — or if the BB thing returned and somehow talked to it — any advantage they had would be gone. So precautions moved from just watching the road to keeping their eyes on the sky and perimeter as well. They were determined not to let the BB back inside, because its presence would prove they had a leak. A spy among them.

Hence the thoughts of dying. The way it seemed to Lawrence, if the aliens wanted to kill them, there was very little chance now that events would unfold in any other way. Their fates were in alien hands.

And Lawrence would bet that there was more in play than that, too. Margaret and Kristina kept trading covert glances. Todd kept looking back at them both from the passenger seat while Dennis drove the second leg. Lisa had even asked, during one silent round of eye-tag, what was going on, as something was definitely happening. But of course everyone had said the same thing.

Nothing.

Lawrence reached for Joanna's hand to find hers was already moving his way. He looked into her eyes and found himself unable to read what he saw.

Was she forgiving him for anything he did, while apologizing for her part in what happened?

Was she saying she loved him after all?

It could be either, or some variant of both. It really didn't matter. Maybe she still didn't want to end this married, but at least they wouldn't end their lives mired in hate. Even if he didn't win a wife, Lawrence at least had his friend back.

As if agreeing with his thoughts, Joanna squeezed his hand and smiled.

"Um … Todd?" Dennis said from the driver's seat.

Todd had been looking around and looking back, instead of fixing his gaze straight ahead. But Dennis sounded worried, and everyone perked up with his query.

There was a long fence ahead strewn with official-looking signs, except they said things that official signs shouldn't say — about shooting on sight, about the laws of Nevada being secondary to military law here, and so on.

That and what almost looked like an ice cream truck at the gate, with three figures standing outside holding long somethings that looked like thick vaulting poles.

"Shit," said Todd.

Lawrence felt his stomach drop and his fear of death slither closer. He'd been pretty sure an ice cream truck wasn't an official military vehicle appropriate to Area 51, but Todd's tone underlined it.

Of course this wasn't the welcome party they'd been hoping for.

Of course these particular folks belonged to the world *outside* the fence.

"Maybe they're just trying to get into the compound," Joanna hoped out loud. "Maybe they're on our side?"

Lawrence didn't think so — or, perhaps more accurately, he thought these might be the kind of people who weren't on anyone's side. Evidence for this came from what he saw happening ahead. Now closer, it looked like they might be holding rocket launchers, aimed at their group instead of the complex. Area 51's apparent antagonists now seemed perfectly willing to be their enemies as well. Opportunists to the core.

"Turn back," Todd said.

"Did you hear from your cousin?"

"I haven't had a signal since Vegas."

"Check anyway!" Dennis shouted.

He slowed the vehicle, but the road was one lane and had a runoff ditch on either side. Flipping a bitch wouldn't be easy, but stopping completely felt worse.

Todd picked up his phone, plugged into the truck's USB drive. From time to time Lawrence had thought hard at that phone, attempting the Jedi Mind Trick to get it to ding with a new notification, specifically a confirmation from Cousin Paulie that he'd gotten Todd's message and it was A-OK to cross the gate and come on in.

But that was yesterday, and today's society was suffering exponential decay. They'd be back in the stone ages by next weekend — the stones were already waiting.

"Nothing."

"It's … It's okay, right?" said Dennis. "This is an *armored* car."

New people streamed from the truck. Three of them. Running forward, yelling something. Dennis slammed the brakes, looked into his side mirrors, and made a noise of resignation as he threw the car into reverse. He looked into the side mirrors once more as he floored it, but then he hit the brake again just as fast.

"Double shit."

"What?" John asked Dennis, looking around. The truck's rear was a vault without any windows.

"More behind us."

"It's a trap!" said Lisa.

"Calm down." Kristina. "These idiots look capable of a *trap* to you?"

On cue, one of the people coming at them from the front tripped and fell. Lawrence winced. He thought the man's rocket might go off.

Instead, something came from the one beside it. He'd aimed right at them and pulled whatever those things had for a trigger.

Lawrence braced for impact. He was pleased to see that his instinct wasn't to run and save himself — not that he could — but instead he kept hold of Joanna's hand.

Might as well go together.

But the rocket didn't strike them, soaring an arc over the armored car's roof, and dragging a pristine white vapor trail behind it.

One.

Two.

And then an explosion detonated somewhere behind them. Not a big, showy movie explosion. It didn't force their ride into the air or tip sideways in the ensuing shockwave. Instead there was a thick **POPPING**, most of the noise muffled by the truck's armored walls.

Lawrence felt a jolt, then felt his heartbeat, and finally found enough voice to speak. "They're firing at the people behind us."

"No shit?" Kristina asked. "You're a genius! **DRIVE!**"

"Where?" Dennis barked. "There's nowhere to go!"

Kristina must not have agreed with this. She shoved Joanna and John aside, wedged herself between the two up front, then seized the wheel from Dennis.

She wrenched it hard right, causing the vehicle to tip toward the culvert but at an angle, almost putting them on their side.

Lawrence braced and saw Lisa do the same, but the rest of his perception was lost to chaos. There was shouting and worried shrieks, then a moment later they were off-roading on the ditch's other side.

"Don't stop don't stop *don't stop!*" Kristina to Dennis, who was still in the driver's seat, despite her intrusion.

They'd been splitting duties for the last few seconds, her taking the steering with him handling velocity and brake. They'd begun to whir and slow. Dennis eased off in response to a rocking and shifting and stalling of their heavier-than-typical cargo.

"DON'T STOP!" Kristina bellowed.

Dennis again pressed the accelerator, but the truck came to a stand-still, its wheels spinning in desert sand.

"What the *FUCK*, Dennis!"

"You were steering!"

"You can't slow down on bad ground! Everyone knows that!"

Todd was up in a second, not pushing Kristina away so much as throwing her down. She glowered up at him while everyone glared in his direction. The action had the feel of a full-body outburst, like screaming obscenities in church.

"Who are you?" Todd said, teeth bared.

"Wh—?"

The entire truck rocked. Something struck just in front of them, blowing dirt and debris across the windshield. They were suddenly in mostly-darkness, no eyes yet adjusted after the bright sun. Bodies fell.

Lawrence felt someone glance down his knees then hit the deck as if shot, but that couldn't be, could it?

"Open the back."

Barely-held calm. Lawrence didn't know whose voice it was.

"OPEN THE BACK!"

A new noise came from overhead — not the whistle of a rocket, but a low hum like the whir of a drone. Absent visuals, Lawrence's mind painted horrible pictures — the warring parties that'd surrounded them now turning a mutual attack on their vehicle ... which must look to the outside world like a rolling bank. Money still meant something. The aliens had only been on Planet Earth for a few days. They must seem like a walnut to these people. A full-on assault was a smart way to get the sweet meat inside.

The back door opened.

The explosion out front hadn't damaged the latch like Lawrence worried it might — this thing was a tank. He wondered if leaving it was the right choice ... should they maybe stay inside?

But no, of course not. They'd be safe only until

the others found a way to blow the lid, and they had artillery to do it.

Lawrence looked up.

Joanna had opened the door. She threw it wide then jumped out, and Lawrence lost all thoughts of staying inside. He went to chase her, but she was still right there by the door's side, holding it open for the others.

Lisa jumped out next, then Margaret and John. Kristina, followed by Dennis. Todd brought up the rear, still staring daggers at the Comedian.

They were on the leeward side of the battle, both combatant parties above the truck on its other side.

"Run?" John taking a poll.

"Wait!"

Lawrence looked. Lisa was pointing toward the base — toward Area 51. The sound he had taken for a drone was actually a helicopter. Some of what he'd taken to be other engines were Army-green Jeeps now spilling from the gate.

But it wasn't going to end that easily.

The ice cream truck thing — if it was, indeed, an ice cream truck — hadn't been waiting at the gate to trap them. The idea was absurd, because why would any humans trap them? It made much more sense that they'd been planning a raid like the one their own group had in mind, but without an inside hookup.

Or, more likely, *both* tribes had come to Area 51 with intent to explode their way inside. Fortunately or unfortunately for Lawrence's group, they had opted to blow each other to smithereens instead of working as a team.

Apparently Todd was wrong. Apparently not everyone was fooled by Area 51's tourist entrance versus its real one. Including Area 51 itself, which appeared to have effectively marshaled its forces.

A rocket streaked through the sky, landing at the foot of one of the Jeeps as it came through the gate. A plume of hard-packed dirt flew into the air, but the driver was undaunted and didn't slow a whit.

Gunfire coughed, then more of it. Coming from both directions now, and at least one of the three fighting forces beyond them hadn't forgotten about the fourth party in the armored truck, because the metallic ping of rounds striking the vehicle made them all duck back. Even after they did, bullets pocked the ground.

More explosions. More gunshots. It seemed to last forever.

Lawrence looked to Joanna, who seemed

suddenly so strong — certainly not looking for *him* at all — and saw a grim determination there.

There was shouting, shooting, a bigger explosion.

More shooting. Then silence.

"I think it's over." Dennis stepped out of cover, to the stalled car's side.

There was a yell. He shouted back, raising his arms.

A second bellow came from a different location, then a third from the first, followed by a whistling rocket.

Lisa shrieked as Dennis blew to pieces.

More shouting.

More gunshots.

Lawrence looked along the truck's body, at the six remaining members of their little party. His heartbeat had landed in his temples. His brain was all out of oxygen.

John shook his head to communicate silently to the rest of them — *Nobody move.*

Footsteps approached. The helicopter was still whirring above, but decreasing in volume as if moving away.

"Todd Cavelli?"

The shout came from the truck's blind side.

Everyone looked at Todd. He shook his head in tiny little movements: *Todd's not here, man.*

"Is Todd Cavelli back there?"

John's forehead wrinkled. His lips half-pursed in a miniature frown. He shifted to rise, and Lisa whispered, *"Don't!"*

But John did. Nobody shot him, so Lawrence leaned away from the truck to peek as well. He saw three soldiers holding guns. The road above them was smoking in two separate places.

"Are you Todd Cavelli?" the lead soldier tried for the third time.

Todd had emerged, tentative. After an uncertain swallow, he said, "I am."

The soldier nodded. The two behind him were already waving to one of the vehicles above, two men responding with a stretcher held between them.

"Paul Cavelli got your message."

FOURTEEN

The Base

KRISTINA WAS PLAYING eye-war with Todd.

It had been an hour since they'd passed Area 51 security and been ushered into what she was quite sure was a forbidden inner sanctum under normal circumstances. The event had an obnoxious effect on Todd. He was vindicated. It was his idea, his persistence, his faith, and ultimately his cousin who'd ushered them to safety.

Kristina kept trying to look his way, but it seemed like he was staring back at her more and more often. The few times when he wasn't, Kristina saw a disturbing sense of satisfaction. His posture and body language were different, now that of a man in charge, a man whose stubborn confidence had finally been rewarded. He struck her as the kind of guy who'd use his power to get more. The kind of guy on whom self-satisfaction was dangerous.

So she walked away. The facility was arranged in rings of tiered security — something Kristina thought might have something to do with the more mundane necessities of life on a top-secret base. There were generals and world-changers, sure, but people here needed to eat, piss and shit, and have their trash cans emptied and hallways swept. The idea of janitors having higher security clearance than some government officials was bizarre yet somehow logical. Generals wouldn't want to scrub all those toilets. The Lucky's group had apparently been gifted that lower tier of security. They had already learned enough secrets to make her hair stand on end, but not enough to blow things with the Russians. Yet.

There'd been no talk of how long they could stay, but judging by the hangars and grounds above as well as the sprawl she'd seen on the official Area 51's footprint — which this "real" Area 51 apparently used — suggested it wasn't just an alien facility, but a functional air base as well. Many of the men and women stationed here seemed to have been assigned elsewhere or fled, leaving plenty of bunks and even a room with a pool table, ping-pong, and an aging Ms. Pac-Man cabinet. They were free to stay, she assumed, or wander until some brush-cut with a stoney expression told her to go back and stay seated. So far, none had.

Kristina thought as she wandered, trying to assimilate their turn of events. She hadn't planned on getting this far. She'd assumed they would be refused at the gate, blown away while standing in front of it, find the place deserted, or get slaughtered along the way. Finding herself inside a military base as hoped — and one that proved conspiracy theorists correct — would take some adjusting.

Same for what she and Margaret had talked about. At first Kristina thought the old woman was crazy. Then she realized she'd wanted to think Margaret was nuts because the alternative was even nuttier.

So … what? She was psychic? She could hear some of what the others were thinking if she focused, and if those thoughts were especially loud? It was the stuff of fantasy. Margaret's implications about the aliens were even more troubling. It was true that Kristina was the odd woman out here.

She'd always been the black sheep, so why would an apocalypse be any different?

Still, she couldn't quite square it all with the idea of herself as a tool. Of herself as a conduit through which alien minds might be able to see. She now understood her thoughts about Heather Hawthorne — an indication not that she was connected to Heather ... but more that Heather, and her ex-husband Meyer, were *also* connected to the aliens.

This wasn't about Heather at all. It was about the fact that several people out there were windows through which the aliens could peek.

You could be the spy, Margaret had said.

Kristina didn't like that way of seeing things, since it implied her own culpability. She may have opened the door that was now wide inside her — she'd taken ayahuasca to experience the universal mind, after all — but the whole thing had been a lark. She'd had a rich friend at boarding school who graduated to become an even richer attorney, and before their relationship soured, that ex-friend had invited Kristina on a yacht ride into international waters with a shaman named Juha.

They'd all drank. They'd all puked. And after that, Kristina had touched the stars.

It was supposed to be a goof. A fun time. When people got high, they said all sorts of things, "I saw God/Aliens/The Flying Spaghetti Monster," among them. That didn't mean they actually did.

But perhaps Kristina had.

She had no way of being sure, but still she'd become possessed by the idea that her internal gossip was right — Meyer Dempsey really was cheating on his current wife with Heather, and the two of them had taken the drug together, more than once. They were windows, and so was she.

Which meant that whether Kristina liked it or not, maybe she *was* the spy.

Should she lock herself in a windowless room?

Should she shut her ears when anyone spoke?

Should she don a blindfold?

Kristina had no idea how this thing worked. Except maybe she did.

Since denying everything to Margaret — bitch didn't need to tell *Kristina* who she was, right or not — her mind hadn't stopped poking at the concept. She'd found its corners and, unless her internal guidance was wrong, she felt sure she had more control than a simple window should afford her. Kristina could close the drapes on that window.

She'd been concentrating, and it seemed to be working so far.

Though, of course, that could all be part of the ruse.

"Excuse me, Miss Fine?"

Kristina turned around. One of the soldiers from earlier was behind her in a light gray hallway.

"Yes?"

He gestured with one arm. "If you wouldn't mind coming with me."

THE COLONEL'S name was Boufat. Kristina kept wanting to make jokes.

"I hope you'll pardon the whirlwind of this all," Boufat said, standing at the small room's front. "The situation requires that we make certain allowances in our protocols, given the state of affairs."

Kristina wanted to roll her eyes, but she'd be the only one. The others were taking this all in like sheep. Military guys talked like a bunch of robots, and yet everyone simply accepted it. They weren't even well-spoken robots — just jargon and junk words.

"Normally we have a lengthy set of testing,

background checks, and requirements for situations involving an increase of security clearance. However, I can inform you that many of our lines to HQ have been cut off and the status of POTUS is unknown. Those in command of this installment feel it's incumbent upon us to risk exposing the seven of you to confidential material in the interest of advancing greater knowledge of this situation."

Kristina raised her hand. The colonel nodded. "Will we be permitted to declassify the status indications of various referential entities incumbent upon completion of our target objectives?"

Boufat paused, puzzled. "I am sorry, ma'am. I do not believe I understand your question."

"Shut up, Kristina," said John.

Boufat waited to see if there was more, then continued.

"As the public has surmised, and as you no doubt have heard through certain widely-accepted channels, this airbase has indeed recovered past evidence of extraterrestrial visits. Our current extraterrestrial guests conform to what we have seen in that prior evidence. This is the same race, in other words."

"That's good," said Joanna.

Nobody responded.

"We believe there is evidence of extrasensory manipulation incumbent upon us, and resident in these individuals."

"He means the aliens are psychic," Todd translated.

"We have suspected for the entirety of this installation's existence that such extrasensory abilities are at the root of their knowledge. They know us, in other words, because one of two things are true. Either they are able to read human minds, or there are sleeper agents among us — aliens in disguise, basically — with whom they are in contact."

Todd was staring at Kristina.

"It is imperative that we answer this question, now that the extraterrestrials have arrived. Or *returned*, as the case may be. And for that reason, we would like to ask for your cooperation."

"With what?" John asked. It was the first real question or comment.

Boufat nodded. "Mr. Cavelli informs us that you have been through one of their stone lines and experienced certain mental changes as a result. With your consent, we would like to test those changes."

The group was starting to nod, but Kristina got

the feeling that testing would happen with or without their consent.

Now they wore badges. Kristina felt like James Bond. Or Jill Bond. Why weren't there any famous female agents? Kim Possible was only a kid, and kind of annoying.

Boufat stopped them outside a chamber with windowed walls. The door was solid, but they'd already seen the alien bodies inside, laying on slabs.

"The aliens, which we have dubbed 'Astrals' in honor of the software that revealed their approach, appear to have one of three forms. The one you brought us, like the subjects in this room, we call 'Titans.' There is also a larger and much more aggressive form we call 'Reptars.'" I understand you are also familiar with them."

The group nodded grimly.

"It is our belief that there is a third form, though we can only infer its existence. This third kind, if it does indeed exist, we call 'Divinity.' This class never seems to leave the motherships." He gestured. "We have recovered remains of two Reptar-class aliens, but they have been dead for a very long time. This is a good thing, at least for now. We have, in the past, recovered several living Titans. They occasionally visit between occupations such as this one. Yours will be our sixth living Titan, in addition to several bodies."

"So you didn't need the one we had," Todd said.

"No, sir. It was not your alien that interested us. It was your mention of the stones."

"You wanted us, not it," John said.

"That is correct. But please, rest assured that we will not vivisect you." There was a long pause. Then Boufat, with the same zero inflection, said, "That was a joke."

Being a professional joke-teller, Kristina hated cracks like that. Normally, the fact that something was a joke meant the opposite was true — which in this case meant they *would* be dissected while still alive. It was sloppy form.

Some in the group offered an uncomfortable laugh, but Lisa alone looked horrified. She went to the window, looked in at the aliens on the slabs, then seemed to notice what Kristina already had: The aliens inside were hooked to monitors. Their chests, despite massive autopsy wounds were rising and falling.

"They're *alive?* Those ones are *alive* while you do that to them?"

"Yes, ma'am," said Boufat without a trace of irony. He'd told them before he'd worked here for years. The man was apparently numb to it.

Lisa started to say something else, but Boufat spoke again before she could.

"Right this way, please, and watch your step."

MORE ROOMS. More aliens. Suits in glass cases and dismantled weaponry. Boufat seemed to have top-secret diarrhea, unable to stop spilling confidential information after that first secret had been uncorked. His revelations fascinated the others, but they made Kristina nervous.

"Why?" Margaret asked later. They'd split off at break time, not because Kristina wanted to but because she needed someone to hear her concerns, and Margaret was the only one who seemed to know anything at all. "Why does it bother you that he showed us everything?"

"Because we're civilians. We're not supposed to know this stuff. Haven't you ever seen a UFO conspiracy show?"

They were in what looked like a break room.

Kristina had a hard time believing that every inch of a place like this wouldn't be wired for sound, but she had no choice. They couldn't go outside to speak — polite men with loaded weapons had put a kibosh on that.

Margaret shifted in her chair. "Boufat said we had to know, to do what he wants us to do."

"But ALL of it? Why did we need to know about their weapons?"

"Who cares?"

"You'll think I'm paranoid."

"I've thought that since I met you. Who do you think you're talking to?"

That's right. Margaret was the Cynic. Maybe this wouldn't be so hard. "You know there are organizations in the government that they won't even let the president see, right?"

"So say the conspiracy nuts."

"*Well?* We can know, but not the president? Doesn't that bother you? These people operate outside the law. What seems more likely? That they'll ask for our help, thank us, then send us on our way? Or that they'll kill us?"

Margaret's face became less smug, less joking.

"I'm not the only one who thinks it. Larry does, and—"

"Lawrence?"

"And John. And Lisa."

"You've talked to them?"

Kristina tapped her head. "I just know. And that's another thing. I swear I can *hear* the aliens in here. They're in pain. Severe pain."

"So what?" Margaret said. "Remember how they keep killing us?"

"If they don't mind keeping aliens in pain for years and years, what might they do to us if it helps them learn a little more?"

"You're being paranoid."

"Yes, I am. Join me, will you?"

They sat in silence.

"There's more," Kristina said. "These aliens. I think they form a collective mind. I think that's why I opened a door when I took ayahuasca. People say it lets you contact the universal consciousness. I thought it was horse shit, but I swear that's how these guys work. The individuals have their own minds, I think, but they do most of their thinking in a group."

"You're sure of this?"

"I'm not sure at all. I'm trying to trust my gut, like you said. 'Don't overthink it.'"

"I didn't think you liked my suggestions. You

told me the ayahuasca was no big deal."

"Yeah. I told you a lot of things."

The implications hung in the air, and then all the truths between them settled.

"Anyway, when they let us go back to our rooms, I sat down like some dumb hippie fruit and tried to still my mind. Like meditation." Kristina made a face. "I started to get that feeling again that they're all connected. That's when I realized there's pain there, too. The ones here call themselves 'the Separated,' and it hurts them. To be apart from the others."

"Again, *So what?*"

"They keep them repressed somehow. It's not that I feel for the aliens, though honestly, it's hard to go that deep and not feel it a little. I wouldn't want to be cut up while I was alive, kept from my family and friends."

"If you don't want to be vivisected," Margaret said, "maybe don't invade other people's planets."

"My point isn't about them. Or at least not directly about them. My point is, they have a natural psychic connection to the others, or at least they *would* have one if they weren't being … I don't know, injected with something?"

"Are you suggesting we free them? So the Big Bad Area 51 people don't cut us up, too?"

"I'm suggesting we keep our options open. And if necessary, maybe we don't free them, but we give the others — the ones outside, still in their ships — a way to *see.*"

FIFTEEN

The Rotunda

ON THEIR SECOND day at Area 51, after a whole lot of briefings and a few college-psychology-style ESP tests involving cards with designs on the back, there was a knock on Todd's door.

He looked at Lawrence, but his assigned room-mate didn't so much as lift his head. After a second knock, Todd said, "Who is it?"

Lawrence looked over. "What?"

The door didn't open. The knock repeated.

"Come in," Todd said.

"Who are you talking to?" Lawrence asked.

Todd stood, walked to the door, opened it, and found Hayward outside, still bleeding from both gunshot wounds.

"'Bout time," Hayward said.

"How are you here?" Todd hadn't seen him since the rocks outside the convenience store.

"Is someone out there?" Lawrence asked.

Todd left the room, let the door close behind him, then began to walk beside Hayward.

"Can we talk?" Hayward asked.

"I don't know." He looked meaningfully at a hallway security camera. "*Can* we talk?"

"There's no sound. Only video."

"Are you sure?"

"*You're* sure," said Hayward.

"How am I sure?"

"Because the Titans are sure."

"So this really *is* their trap? This really *is* their plan? The aliens set this up?"

Hayward gave Todd a look that suggested he was embarrassed for him. "You know better than that by now."

They walked.

"What did you want to talk about?" Aware that nobody else could see Hayward, Todd kept his lips tight and mumbled so the cameras wouldn't think he was having a conversation with himself.

"We've been here longer than we expected," Hayward said.

"That's good, though, right?"

Hayward shrugged. It made his chest wound squelch like a stepped-on sponge. "You think so. Others are starting to get restless."

"Why?"

"They think they're prisoners."

"That's ridiculous. We're guests." But now that Todd thought about it, he wouldn't truly know the difference unless he tried to leave.

"Sure. But that's exactly why you need to hear what I have to say."

"Todd! Todd!" Someone was behind him, rushing.

"Tell me quick."

"No worries," said Hayward. "You already know."

Todd allowed Lawrence to drag him away as he explained the colonel wanted to see everyone. They ended up in a large, perfectly round room that appeared to be coated in tinfoil — the Rotunda. The space was a parabolic dome with a vent at the very top. Taking up maybe a fifth of the total floor space — and unlike the other times they'd been called to the same room — three of the Titans were before them on lock-wheeled rolling stretchers.

Todd thought the one on the left was the alien they'd brought with them, but he couldn't be sure. All seven members of the Lucky's crew were at the feet end of the stretchers, with Boufat between them and the extraterrestrials.

"As I explained when you arrived, you are the first humans we've found who have gone through an alien formation and come out mentally altered, yet still alive."

"Comforting," said Margaret.

"It seems the Astrals can tune their stones to conduct a number of functions. A line like the one you crossed is thus far the rarest. We didn't realize the Vegas line was capable of creating survivors. We believed it to be what we call a fatality line. The fact that so many of your number made it through suggests that either you were all extremely fortunate — all seven of you—"

Eight, Todd thought. Until Dennis died, there'd been eight.

"—or the Astrals *allowed* you to pass. In any case, that makes you very interesting to us and our study of the Astrals."

Todd looked at the alien bodies. They'd heard this speech before, but it was always followed by assertions that they'd get to actual human-alien tests "eventually." To Todd, who was eager to try, it had sounded an awful lot like a parent saying "we'll see" to stopping for ice cream. Such things always meant no.

"We have repressed long-range psychic function in the subjects here so that this place can remain invisible to the Astrals," Boufat continued, "but doing so entails certain risk. To the chase, we are concerned if we attempt psychic contact while keeping them mostly psychically repressed, it might kill the subjects. That is why we have only brought out half of our living cohort. Well, slightly less, as you have graciously increased our live compliment to seven."

Boufat was giving him the shivers. He'd said the subjects might die, but technically the humans here were subjects, too. He'd said their live compliment was seven — the same number as the folks from Lucky's.

"Block it out," Hayward said.

Todd turned. He'd just noticed his old friend, bringing their count to eight. He couldn't answer while in a group, so he waited for more.

"Those are *her* worries, not yours," Hayward clarified. "You're all connected, remember? So block it out."

Todd knew where Hayward meant.

He looked at Kristina, then away when she glanced back.

With a feeling like tightening an internal fist, Todd blocked it out.

"In any event," Boufat said, "we would like to commence. So if you wouldn't mind arranging yourself around the aliens, two or three per Titan, and preparing your minds to …"

"Why now?" John asked.

"Pardon?"

"If you think it might kill them — and if you've been saying that you'd need lots of time, to be sure — why are we trying this now?"

"Please." Boufat sighed. "It's time to get going."

The Threat

"Moscow."

Margaret considered Kristina. They'd talked a lot so far at Area 51, increasingly secure in the notion that they weren't being overheard. After all those chats, Margaret had mostly lost her fear of the other woman's bite. Kristina had softened a little at Lucky's, then a lot at Area 51, thanks to an acute fear she couldn't repress. She'd been right about Kristina — the drug she'd taken nearly a decade ago had given her access to the planet's emotional firehose, whereas Margaret and the others were only in contact with other minds in the group — and even then, only intermittently, when the broadcaster was mentally shouting.

Kristina, on the other hand, was connected much deeper. She assimilated information from all over, and it was more terrifying for the fact that she usually had no idea where it was coming from.

"What?"

"That's the reason they're pushing these tests. Moscow's been attacked."

"Attacked?"

"To put it mildly." Kristina described fighter jets, an impatient and terrified government, a nuclear weapon, and swift retaliation from the mothership above the city. It was ashes now. Basically a pit.

"We already know there've been all sorts of abductions," Kristina said. "Thousands and thousands."

"Right."

"But very little open hostility. Every time there's been a report of an attack, humans seem to have struck first."

"You said Moscow struck first. The humans, I mean."

"Yes. But if you think the US government is going to explain it away as, 'Well, the Russians cast the first stone,' you're mistaken. They see it as an act of war, bet your ass."

"So you think they're having us try to talk to the Titans because …"

"Because time's up."

They both nodded. It should have been scarier, but they were mostly scared out.

"That means time's up for us, too. What did you feel when you were in there trying to contact the Titans?"

"Nothing," Margaret said.

"Same. They're not partially repressed. They're entirely repressed. I feel so much now, but I felt nothing from them."

"And?"

"They gave us three of the old ones. I couldn't explain how, but I'm sure the Titan we brought in wasn't one of the three we saw. The old ones are weak. They'll probably give us the other four next, and our boy will be one of them. Maybe we'll be able to contact him because he's newer and hasn't been on their drugs for years, but I think we should talk about what happens if we can't."

"Why?"

"Have you heard all the activity on the surface?"

Margaret nodded. They all had. Their quarters were on subterranean level two, but the big domed building, judging by its size and the fact that it was one floor up, almost had to brush the surface. It was quiet, the first time they'd seen the room. But now, they heard constant clamor — jets taking off and landing, the heavy clank of machinery being moved or assembled.

"I think they were content to wait and take their time at first, but they're gearing up now Moscow has forced their hand."

"And you're sure about Moscow?"

Kristina nodded. "I saw it."

"You can see that far?"

"I think I saw it through someone else's eyes. Maybe someone who did ayahuasca once, and I can tap into them or whatever, since they'd be 'open' like me. They saw the Moscow thing on television."

"Where?"

"I don't know." Kristina shook her head. "They

were somewhere dark. Concrete walls and no windows. It was dressed up, but it felt to me like a bunker."

"Heather? Heather Hawthorne?"

Kristina said nothing. Margaret nodded.

"I think they'll give us another shot with the remaining four Titans," Kristina continued. "It only makes sense, and why not after all the work they did here? But after that? I get the feeling the time for communication and diplomacy might be over. They'll be much more interested in blowing each other up now."

"Okay," said Margaret, trying to assimilate it all. She believed what Kristina said. She had enough insight into the other woman's mind that she'd be a fool not to.

"We need to decide what to do if they give up on us. We need to have a plan for what happens if they decide not to let us go."

"Do you have a suggestion?" Margaret asked.

"Yes." Then she told her.

Margaret took a few deep breaths, then made herself stand so she wouldn't fall over. She tried to focus, to hold it all together. Then she nodded. "Okay. What should we tell the others?"

"Nothing. We can't risk talking to everyone. They'll just have to do their best."

"Their best to *what?*"

"To get out of the way."

That was an understatement. It didn't make Margaret feel any better, but it wasn't like they had any options.

"There's something else. I don't think it's important yet … but I think it will be. Months from now, maybe."

Margaret tried not to flinch at the idea of seeing the future. She trusted whatever was inside Kristina now — the first time she'd had faith in anything for a very long time — and supposed if it wasn't fortune-telling, then it was probably a long computation of inevitable logic. The coming of something that, given current circumstances lined up like dominoes, couldn't help but be.

"If it's Heather's eyes I'm seeing through," Kristina said, "then her ex-husband's been abducted."

"A lot of people have been abducted."

"Not like this."

"What do you mean?" Margaret asked.

"The Astrals … they call him the first of The Nine."

SIXTEEN

The Push

BACK IN THE Rotunda later that day, Kristina got a distinct feeling of laxity from every single military person including Boufat. They'd been so rigid, so set on procedure and protocol. On entry, each of them submitted to a palm scan and an ID check. John would enter, the door would close, then Lisa would submit to the same checks and be allowed to enter, and so on down the line. Boufat spoke formally enough to sound like a joke. They all got *sirs* and *ma'ams*. It was like being served by high-class waiters with serious trust issues.

The laxity — that sense of no protocol, no pointless, ritualistic bullshit — was frightening. Kristina had shed most of her sarcasm, becoming someone she didn't particularly like for all her weakness. The Kristina who entered the Rotunda that last time was the weakest of all. And not remotely funny. She couldn't have cruelly severed some asshole at the knees with an insult if she'd tried.

Boufat was a shadow of his former self. "Okay. These are the other four Titans. You know what to do."

It was true. They did know what to do. Even before this morning, the Army — or whoever ran this spook show — had set them up in this very same room, hooked to video monitors and computers that supposedly mimicked what they understood of the Astral mind and the Titans' anticipated responses. This morning, working with real Titans, had been mostly the same. They'd had many hours of training, and thus didn't need the lecture. But that wasn't the point. Boufat *always* delivered it. Now he looked like he was going through the motions, instead of this being the most important lecture in history.

For shit's sake, his uniform wasn't even fully buttoned.

"John, Joanna." He pointed at the first alien. "Kristina, Lisa." The second. And so on down the line, leaving Lawrence as the only person left unpaired with his alien. All alone just like in real life, because Joanna thought he was a douchebag.

Oh, look! Her insults weren't gone after all, they were just now on the nose.

She looked at Margaret, paired with Todd. She'd seen the laxity, too, and knew what it meant. Nobody expected much of this test. This was only perfunctory. They'd try it, then probably burn the room, then get back to building warheads.

"Begin," Boufat said.

TODD CAUGHT the look between Margaret and Kristina.

It warped his focus, and Margaret was left to try mindfucking the alien all by her lonesome. Would she notice? Frankly, Todd could give less than a shit.

"Look at them," said Hayward beside him. "They're up to something."

Todd nodded to (no one) Hayward. They knew that already.

"It might be up to you," Hayward said.

Todd wanted to confer, but there was no way and no time. He only knew that Area 51 was their only hope and Kristina and Margaret, for reasons unknown, were planning to get them expelled.

Why would they do that, unless Kristina was a rat? He'd worked out that she was a spy, but for the first time he was starting to suspect she might be an *actual* spy. Maybe she was working for the Iraqis. The Saudis. Who else might spy on America? Were the Russians still a threat?

Or was it the aliens? Boufat himself had raised the idea of alien sleeper agents hiding among the human population. He hadn't said it like a real thing, but like the ridiculous notion you dismiss on your way to a true conclusion. Was it possible? Maybe Todd had figured out something even the illustrious Area 51 had not.

"Todd," said John, noticing his gaze. He tipped his head toward the alien. Not one of their psychic readouts was lighting up. "Eyes on the prize."

Nothing.

There was nothing.

As Kristina feared, the aliens at Area 51 had been sucked dry like spent oranges. Lobotomized, same as anyone held in tight quarters for so long. It wasn't even institutionalized, like with long-term prisoners, because there was no society here for them — no alternative way of life for them to build.

Psychic beings who'd been psychically neutered, prevented even from communing with each other. Trapped in tiny cells, cut open repeatedly, then sewn up and returned to isolation.

Kristina, despite her best intentions, couldn't help but feel for them. They bled when they were cut. They had heartbeats and breathed air — maybe or maybe not oxygen, but Earth air just the same. They even looked like giant humans. So when she reached into their minds and found only dust, Kristina couldn't help but empathize. It could be her on the slab, or any of them.

Look at you, said her mother's voice. *Weak and emotional, after all.*

She pushed it away.

Mother had no place here.

She had no place anywhere, in Kristina's life, anymore.

She looked to the Titan to her left, reaching out to it instead. There was nothing. Then to the other two for more of the same.

Boufat and the other military folks were watching the displays, seeing flatlines again, conferring with one another.

Time's almost up.

But she needed to figure out which one was

their Titan, to do what she'd planned. Maybe they'd cut him off like the others, but that was okay. She had a line to him, and he'd have a line to the other Titans.

Their minds had grown weak, but she could still feel that seed of potential within them. She'd been meditating regularly, hating herself for being airy but believing she understood at least this part of how they worked.

The collective mind was their fuel, the individuals almost like limbs. They only needed a hole to be poked. She thought she knew what'd happen next — that, she'd seen as well, though through whose eyes she could not say — but it was still somewhat up in the air.

There was a chance Kristina connected the dots and still nothing happened.

She couldn't make a move until she knew which Titan was the newest and least damaged by being here. Their Titan could be any of the four, but she had neither time nor strength to try each one.

They weren't exactly the same, but the differences were slight to her very human eyes.

Why hadn't she taken a picture?

She thought maybe others had, using phones charged inside the armored car. She could have studied it with a photo. Then she might know which Titan to try.

"Okay," Boufat said. "I think we're about done here."

Time's up.

"John. Which Titan's the one we brought here? Do you know?"

He looked over. "Why?"

"Never mind why. Just tell me. *Hurry!*"

He heard her urgency, saw the way she glanced at Boufat … and the way the men around him were reaching for their sidearms.

This was it. She had one stab. One *exactly.*

John pointed at the one on the end without trying to hide what he was doing. "That one."

"Are you sure?"

A heartbeat. The men with guns were two steps closer.

Then, "Yes."

"THAT ONE."

Todd watched John point at one of the Titans. His pulse doubled. This was it.

"Are you sure?"

"Yes."

Kristina turned toward the body at the end, but Todd was already in motion.

He'd pulled out the sliver of snapped-off metal he'd broken from beneath his bed then taped at one end to form a handle. He'd just have to stick her fast. Judging by her intensity, whatever she had in mind would happen fast.

Todd lunged. He made it halfway over the alien he'd been attempting to hurdle on his way to Kristina, but he'd only reached the torso.

The men with guns rushed forward.

John tried to get in the middle, but Todd was too fast. He rolled to the deck, then under the cot.

He had Kristina by the ankle a moment later.

She looked down with fury on her face. "Get off!"

He used the shiv to open a gash in her opposite leg.

Kristina went down, taking the second cot with her. The Titan pounded the floor in an untidy heap.

A buzzer went off. One of the monitors flashed red.

Had it died? Had the Army really milked them to that much frailty?

Shouts. Running.

The Rotunda door burst open. Boufat stuck his head out and yelled. Another was on a radio. Something squawked.

Todd kept his eyes on Kristina, then crab-rushed after her.

AGAIN TODD GOT HER ANKLE.

Kristina didn't bother to shout this time. She just reared back then kicked him in the face. The move required putting all her weight on her copiously bleeding bad leg, so she staggered as Todd grunted and clutched his nose, trying not to fall.

He still had his knife, and the furor was focused at the room's middle, where three cots still stood. She'd felt the fourth die. It'd been like the winking-out of a dim light.

The Titan. She had to reach the Titan.

Kristina ran, trying to rise above the pain. It worked a little, but then she over-sprinted, found herself unable to brake, and went ass-over-teakettle.

She looked ahead. Their Titan was still where they'd left it. But she'd lost her bearings. Was that the one John indicated? She had to believe it was if she expected to keep crawling.

Todd got her ankle again, both of them on the floor now.

Kristina kicked him harder, hearing his nose break. Her ankle broke free, but she'd lost most of her wind, adrenaline now ramping her reality to a flashing, screaming crimson haze. Time slowed and sped up at the same time.

She found her mark.

Kristina stood, then looked down at the Titan. She didn't have to reach it, not really. This was more like opening her own window. If she opened it and let *them* see, then—

Her eyes were wide, trying to take it all in and pass it on.

She was the conduit. She was the window.

But then someone screamed and her gaze jolted away just as she began to feel presence growing on the other end.

"Back away. Nice and slow." Todd had Lisa by the arm, his knife hand at her throat. "Back away or she dies."

Kristina's hands went up. The advancing soldiers with the guns — those already in the room and those still entering through the open door — stopped advancing.

Then Lisa spoke. "Roll the dice."

And her mind sent Kristina a crystal clear image. Little Girl Lisa holding up a tiny fist. *I'm stronger than you think*, it seemed to say. Did she know what Kristina had in mind? They were connected — and Lisa had been deeper inside the alien mind than the rest of them — after all.

Roll the dice.

Her meaning was clear: No individual's life mattered. They were, in a way, their own collective … and losing one of them was better than the rest.

Kristina turned from Lisa focused every molecule of her attention on the Titan, and *pushed*. The only question was whether what she'd seen and believed about the aliens' two earthbound forms was true.

They were interchangeable.

They were the same thing, choosing to take different forms.

And then she knew it was true.

SEVENTEEN

The Collective

THE COLLECTIVE FELT the push and shoved right back.

One of the earthbound windows flew open. The Collective, always watching through its countless eyes, had been waiting, looking, wondering if its intentions would bear fruit.

It knew the humans were hiding something.

When the window opened, the Collective saw its missing fellows.

Three present, three still hidden, one fallen.

It saw the slicing with knives of butchers.

It saw the imprisonment. The isolation. The cutting-off.

It was the apathy. The oh-so-human tendency to ruin. The Archive had told them as much, told them over and over again. The Archive told different tales at the end of each epoch, when they returned to read it, to retrieve it, to reset it and try again.

It sent the push.

And gave the confined ones the means needed to return.

"HOLY SHIT."

Lisa wasn't big on swearing, but she couldn't believe her eyes.

When she'd been little, Mommy had played family movies only from a juke stuffed with censored versions of family favorites. Bleeped words were only semi-tolerable, so Lisa usually saw a dub instead. *Sugar* to cover the filth of a *shit*, but never in a matching voice. The censorship was never mentioned. It was as if Mommy thought she was stupid. As if she might not even notice.

But there was no word better than *shit* for the events unfolding before her.

Something uncorked with that first obscenity, and after that she might as well have had a disorder. Pure profanity, punctuated only by modifiers to make her swearing more severe.

But still Lisa wasn't going out of her mind. She was out of Mommy's clutches and would never go back. She didn't have to be docile like Todd expected.

She would never be a fragile little girl again.

After telling Kristina to roll the dice — she knew Kristina was up to something that required focus on the Titans, but not what — she fell as if fainting and back-elbowed Todd in the balls with all her might.

He might have slit her throat, but that was okay.

Kristina was rolling the dice, and so was Lisa.

She came up seven instead of snake-eyes, and soon Todd was on the floor with his stupid little pig-sticker, moaning.

Then the swearing — not in repulsion, but in awe.

Once it started to happen, she realized she'd seen it before. Deep in the Astral mind, through another kind of window opened by the voice that called itself Stranger. She'd seen this change. This choice and this altering of choice.

Titans and Reptars were not different things.

They were one in the same.

The Titan Kristina had focused on changed first.

Its white body shifted to jet black like the winking-out of a sun. It grew wider and longer at once, its white limbs turning hard and ebony, shiny as if gleaming with polish. The Titan's head swelled. Its mouth opened, soon much larger than its entire head had been before.

The mouth grew teeth — many, *many* teeth in concentric rings.

The stretcher collapsed beneath it.

Its body rolled sideways like a barrel, then towered from the rearmost of its now-many legs, a blue spark in its gut.

The creature purred. Then it screeched.

The Army men fired.

The alien lowered its head and charged, seemingly eyeless but with perfect accuracy. Its new shell must have been impervious because the thing didn't slow a beat as it grabbed the lead soldier in its jaws and wildly shook him.

A snap bisected the body.

Legs landed beside Todd, who screamed and flinched back.

"Go. *GO!*"

Margaret picked up a chair to swing at the military men who weren't even bothering to aim at her. The other two Titans had nearly transformed, invigorated by their renewed access to the collective. She looked at Kristina, just behind Margaret, and wordlessly understood.

Parts of what had happened here, Stranger had shown her, too.

The Reptars were not picky. They seemed to be mindless, like animals, failing or unable to differentiate between friend and foe. Lisa supposed they were neither. She suspected the Astrals had used her group, but now they had used them right back.

Escape meant life.

Staying meant death.

Odds were the same for them all.

And hopefully, the house didn't always win.

The airmen were armed, and that, the Reptars seemed to understand. They rushed the gunmen first, making quick work of them. A few tried to run back through the door, but one of the aliens lunged after them, wedging its huge black body in the frame.

The doorframe buckled. A man screamed. The Reptar freed itself by scrabbling backward with the nearly-escaped man in its mouth.

Margaret's first *Go!* had put them behind a stack of equipment, but the door was the only way out unless they had keycards to open another, which they didn't.

Sirens screamed as ceiling-mounted cherries swirled with amber light.

Lisa watched the warped door try and fail to close.

"Come on," said Kristina.

They skirted the perimeter, making their way around to the door while the Reptars chased someone — Oh, God, it was Joanna — into a curved space that functioned as a corner.

She screamed. The others turned toward her. A second later, Joanna was gone.

Lawrence shouted, but John took him around the waist in a flying tackle.

Momentum threw them both between a pair of huge consoles, and when one of the Reptars tried to follow, it wedged its head as the other had at the door. The backend of the struggling monster was an undiluted nightmare — waving tentacles, a wash of electric blue reflected by the equipment that had to be coming from the creature's throat, maybe along with all those rattles and purrs.

Reinforcements arrived, saw the commotion, and engaged.

They tried to flank the one that'd shredded

Joanna, but it only drew them away from the exit and attracted the attention of the beast attacking Lawrence and John.

The first Reptar turned and roared, a grating purr that shook Lisa's bones.

The military fired machine guns.

The Reptar coughed, spurted fluid, lurched, and fell still.

Apparently their vulnerable spot was the throat — the alien could be killed after all. Lisa, Kristina, and Margaret made for John and Lawrence, who were now emerging.

Then all five went for the door, free of both airmen and monsters.

A shout came from behind. "GET BACK HERE, YOU TRAITOR!"

Lisa heard Todd's yell.

The two remaining Reptars heard it, too, and turned to answer.

SOMEONE HAD GIVEN the order to evacuate and the facility had miraculously complied. Lisa guessed that made sense. In the event of an emergency, you didn't lock people inside. The doors were wide and the way was clear ... until John, Kristina, and

Margaret were occupying the final stairwell with Lawrence holding the door and Lisa assuming the rear.

"STOP!"

Colonel Boufat led a squadron of airmen. All had machine guns, every one of them raised and pointed. He must have escaped, then called for reinforcements.

"I can't let you go. You're too important to the war effort."

"FUCK the war effort," said Lisa, embracing one final swear.

Boufat opened his mouth to respond and his people visibly readied themselves.

But then the cadre was stopped by a cacophony behind them.

They turned and saw the last three Reptars, one with a mangled cell door still hanging from its massive foreleg.

And the war effort no longer mattered.

EIGHTEEN

The Forgetting

"WE HAVE A BIT OF A CONUNDRUM," said the man in black.

John looked up. He would have sworn he was in a jail cell not long ago, but that didn't really make sense. He remembered running from Area 51, and even though it seemed impossible, he also seemed to remember watching his party get frozen by beams of light and sucked into the belly of five different alien shuttles.

His memory of the whole thing was fuzzy, like something experienced in an altered state. And no, that didn't make sense either.

He had to be imagining it. But then how else had he gotten here?

Area 51 was surrounded by desert. There had

been a half-dozen gleaming black aliens eating their way through the military personnel and scientists inside. Even if none of the airmen survived to chase them down, they couldn't possibly have made it all that way on foot. Not without water.

Now the room was a uniform white.

An extremely bright light was in his eyes and he seemed unable to move his head to look away from it. The man in black might not actually be wearing black. It might be some sort of weird light poisoning making him look that way because he was standing behind its source.

John wondered if he'd be able to see again after staring at the sun like this.

Strangely, he wasn't afraid. He had no idea where he was. His mind was foggy, and he'd swear his surroundings kept changing, but none of that felt like any big deal. He was chill, three stiff drinks or so.

All was well with the world, such that the world was these days.

"Oh yeah?" said John.

The man in black clarified. "Not the conundrum you might be imagining."

"I don't know any conundrum."

"I thought maybe you'd heard. It doesn't matter. None of it matters."

The question of a conundrum — one he might have heard of, at that — was very interesting for a little while. Then it floated away and was gone.

"Our conundrum … our problem, if you will, is that five of you survived."

"And that's a problem?"

"We predicted one. Maybe two."

"Survived what?"

"The game."

"What game?"

"You might call it something else. Again it doesn't matter."

And again, that was interesting. Until it wasn't.

"There was trust involved. We had to make certain assumptions."

"*Who* had to make assumptions? Who are you?"

"I'm not who you think."

"I don't *think* anything at all."

"What about Lisa?"

"What about her?"

"She thinks. She knows." Pause. "We've met."

"That's Lisa. Not me."

"You are one. You will always be one, as long as you remember. You recall the stones, do you not?"

John recalled the stones. At the time, the stones had terrified him. Now, in this haze, he could see their true function. They'd made the judgment, like the Archive eventually would.

"That's exactly what I mean," said the man in black.

"What is?"

"You know about the Archive. You know about the Change."

"You mean, I know that the white aliens and the black aliens can transform into each other?"

"Among other things," the man answered.

"Okay. So what?"

"You know. The others know. The stones bonded you. It was known, but we did not think so many would survive."

"Are you with the aliens? With the Astrals?"

"Yes. But I am also something else."

More quiet. More waiting. Still hazy, John found he didn't mind. He'd just become aware of a swishing, sparkling kind of light show in his right-side peripheral vision. Whatever was making all that light was hidden behind a barrier. He couldn't see, no matter how much he tried to contort his sight.

"You see," said the man in black, "Kristina's access now travels two ways. She became aware of her connection to the Collective. We cannot allow this. Not now. Not before the Archive is found."

"What are you talking about?"

"The five of you are connected. In a way, it means you are all aware of the link. It would have been possible to obfuscate it with one survivor. Or two. But with five, the damage to us is too great."

"How the hell does doing something to *us* hurt *you?*"

"You do not understand." But the man in black did not explain. "We have already spoken with the others. We know you made the decision. Without a correct choice, things might have gone as we anticipated. No survivors. One survivor. Maybe two. But we cannot dispose of five. Doing so will cause a ripple."

John tried to decide what should interest him more, this feeling that someone had been watching them the entire time like a human ant farm, or the casual way the man in black was talking about killing them.

"Do you mean the choice of which Titan was ours?"

"Yes. You made the selection. Kristina made the connection. It was flawless."

"It was hardly flawless. We lost Joanna and …"
He stopped. Fuck Todd.

"Grist for the mill."

"Does Lawrence see it that way?"

"Lawrence is whole. He has already found himself, as have all of you."

"What does that mean?"

"It's the root of our conundrum. But again, not *that* kind of conundrum."

"I only know one kind of conundrum," John said.

"And yet you willingly made the choice. How?"

"How what?"

"How did you know which Titan was yours? They are nearly identical. Without an image, you could not know. The drone took precautions to prevent imagery."

"Drone?"

"A flying ball like our shuttles. We know you have seen it."

"It prevented our cameras from working? Because you didn't want us taking a picture of the Titan? Why?"

"The deception was necessary. We had lost six of our own, and they were deeply hidden."

John seemed to remember a military man

saying the aliens didn't know what happened inside Area 51. What was his name? It didn't matter. It seemed to be true. The Astrals had concocted a plan to find out where it was … but so much seemed dependent on chance.

"It was not chance," said the man, seeming again to read his mind. "But it balanced atop free will, which is equally dubious. Particularly a sense of trust that Kristina would do what she did. But your kind is not the only species with faith."

It was a strange idea, a strange thing to say.

"How did you know which one it was?" the man asked.

"I made a guess."

"You guessed correctly."

John shrugged. "Of course. My luck got hot when the world ended. Ballbuster, right?"

"What would you have us do with you, John Abbott?"

John tried again to look around, but his head remained anchored. "Where the hell am I?" Then, bonus question, "Why can't I think straight?"

"Where you are does not matter."

"Sure, it does."

"It does not matter because you can't think straight."

"Oh? And why is that? What did you do to my mind?"

"We have chosen the Forgetting. It is early. You must promise not to remember."

"How the fuck can I promise something like …?" It was too small a question. "What the hell's going on here?"

A new voice spoke. A female, coming from the flashing lights.

"It was never our intention for your connection-bearer to become aware of her connection. Do you know how? Think carefully. Worlds hang in the balance."

"I have no idea." He was growing annoyed. And also hazier. What was this person again? These people? Why couldn't he see them?

"Think quickly, before the Forgetting," said the female voice.

"What did you ask me again?" John asked.

"He is too far down the path," said the female voice.

"Try again," argued the man.

"No." The woman was firm. "Let him go."

The man came closer. John could *almost* see him.

"Listen to me, John Abbott. You cannot be

severed, but you cannot pollute the stream. We have decided to remove all five of you from the stream then let you sleep. You will wake up three years hence, in Heaven's Veil. You will not remember being here, or anything from the last nine days of your life. Do you understand?"

John thought he should protest, but he was getting very sleepy. He barely cared about answers. He remembered being annoyed and frustrated, but that was so long ago. The light was hypnotic. Soothing.

"I understand."

"You will, by the terms in your fiction, live happily ever after. It is required. When you die, you will die one by one, and far apart. It is the only way to sever so many bound so closely."

"Okay." Then, because John felt newly giddy and the idea amused him, he added, "Sounds good to me!"

"You will not know each other. The five of you shall be strangers. You will, of course, naturally gravitate together, but that must happen only after you are already in Heaven's Veil."

"What's Heaven's Veil?"

"It is your home. And when you wake, you will believe you have always lived there. You traveled east, into the mountains. You camped outside the Axis Mundi. Do you understand?"

"All but 'Axis Mundi.'"

"The well. The portal."

"I don't understand."

"You will," said the man. "Lawrence and his wife Joanna did the same, but from another place. Joanna was killed along the way. Lawrence will believe this, and when your micro-collective eventually reforms, he will tell you as much."

"Okay."

"Kristina and Lisa and Margaret, all arriving separately from separate directions, also went to Vail and camped at the Axis. They will believe this, and when you reform, they will tell you as much."

"All right."

"Who are you?"

"John Abbott."

"And what are you?"

"Lucky."

The man paused at that. He seemed to look in the woman's direction.

"Close enough," she said.

The light grew brighter. And brighter. And brighter.

John felt himself drifting into a great white void,

all thoughts of a man in black or a woman among dancing lights forgotten.

He tried to hold the tether of his other thoughts. His friends.

They'd come here together. There were five of them. The man said they'd forget each other, then reform a group years later. He didn't want to forget. He didn't want to let go.

"You believed in us," John said as the last of it faded. "You had to put your trust in humanity."

"We always have. It may not look that way to your kind, but we always have."

"Us," John said as he began to drift again. "It's all about us."

He meant humanity, not himself, but already the idea was fading again into forgetfulness.

"Not about you. This has always been about Meyer Dempsey."

Meyer Dempsey? John knew that name.

Then he didn't know it at all.

His eyes opened. For a few blinks, it felt like he was waking up — and from an extraordinarily long nap at that — *a three year nap*, something inside him said.

It felt like he'd been somewhere else, with other people, in some place when the world was different.

But that feeling passed too, and he sat up in his bed.

He was in Heaven's Veil.

He had work to do. Places to go.

John boiled water for coffee, then opened his front door and took in the enormous blue-glass pyramid of the Apex.

"John?" his wife called.

John turned. *Patty*.

Her name was Patty. He needed the reminder just for a second, and then it was something he'd always known.

"Yes?" he replied.

"Don't you want to take an umbrella? The mothership says it might rain."

John looked up. The mothership had shifted west, and if it rained, Patty was right — he'd get plenty wet.

"I'll take my chances," he told her.

The End...

VEGAS WAS ONLY THE BEGINNING.

Longshot is only a tiny corner of a massive sci-fi

story of conquest … and there's an entire sci-fi epic left to go. Curious who Meyer Dempsey is and what role he plays in Earth's forthcoming change? Curious about the experiments made on humans, why they will determine our fate, and the deep past of aliens on Earth? Want to know the grand plan the Astrals (Reptars, Titans, and the yet-unseen Divinity) have for our planet? Pick up *Invasion: The Complete Series* available now.

They are coming. The countdown has begun...

Enormous spheres are heading toward Earth. They will arrive in six days. Meyer Dempsey knows the time has come to act on the preparations he's made. He knows where he must take his family, if they can make it before society eats itself alive with fear.

Get Invasion today!

A Quick Favor...

If you enjoyed this book, please take a moment to write a short review on your favorite online bookstore so other readers can enjoy it, too.

Thanks so much!
Johnny and Avery

About the Authors

Avery Blake doesn't want you to know where she lives, or what she does. She travels the world, moving from place to place quickly to ensure she can't be tracked. It's safer that way.

When she's not looking over her shoulder, you can find her in the corner of a cafe, facing the exit, typing as fast as she can.

Johnny B. Truant is co-owner of the Sterling & Stone Story Studio, an IP powerhouse focusing on books and adaptations for film and television. It's the best job in the world, and he spends his days creating cool stuff with partners Sean Platt and David W. Wright, as well as more than 20 gifted storytellers.

Johnny is the bestselling author of over 100 books under various pen names, including the Fat Vampire and Invasion series. On the nonfiction side, he's also co-author of the indie publishing mainstay Write. Publish. Repeat. and co-host of the weekly Story Studio Podcast.

Originally from Ohio, Johnny and his family now live in Austin, Texas, where he's finally surrounded by creative types as weird as he is.

Also By Avery Blake

The Invasion Series

Longshot

Invasion

Contact

Colonization

Annihilation

Judgment

Extinction

Resurrection

Save The City Series

Save The City

Save The Girl

Save The World

Stonefall Series

Alienation

Stonefall

Snowfall

Downfall

The Taken Saga

The Taken

The Changed

The Hidden

The Saved

The Next Evolution

Transition

Convergence

Evolution

Stand-Alone Novels

Analog Heart

Family Royale

Ruthless Positivity

Vicarious Joe

Also By Johnny B. Truant

The Dead World Series

Dead Zero

Dead City

Dead Nation

Dead Planet

Empty Nest

The Fat Vampire Series

Fat Vampire

Fat Vampire 2: Tastes Like Chicken

Fat Vampire 3: All You Can Eat

Fat Vampire 4: Harder, Better, Fatter, Stronger

Fat Vampire 5: Fatpocaplypse

Fat Vampire 6: Survival of the Fattest

The Fat Vampire Chronicles

The Vampire Maurice

Anarchy and Blood

Vampires in the White City

The Beam Series

The Beam Season One

The Beam Season Two

The Beam Season Three

Robot Proletariat Series

En3my

Robot Proletariat

The Infinite Loop

The Hard Reset

Cascade Failure

Reboot

The Invasion Series

Longshot

Invasion

Contact

Colonization

Annihilation

Judgment

Extinction

Resurrection

The Tomorrow Gene Series

Null Identity

The Tomorrow Gene

The Tomorrow Clone

The Eden Experiment

Stand Alone Novels

Pretty Killer

Patter Black

Burnout

The Target

CPSIA information can be obtained
at www.ICGtesting.com
Printed in the USA
BVHW031041060223
657971BV00018B/922

9 781629 551739